Frank T. Buckland

Fish Hatching

SALZWASSER
VERLAG

Frank T. Buckland

Fish Hatching

Reprint of the original, first published in 1863.

1st Edition 2022 | ISBN: 978-3-37500-683-9

Verlag (Publisher): Salzwasser Verlag GmbH, Zeilweg 44, 60439 Frankfurt, Deutschland
Vertretungsberechtigt (Authorized to represent): E. Roepke, Zeilweg 44, 60439 Frankfurt, Deutschland
Druck (Print): Books on Demand GmbH, In de Tarpen 42, 22848 Norderstedt, Deutschland

FISH HATCHING.

FISH HATCHING.

BY

FRANK T. BUCKLAND

LONDON

1863.

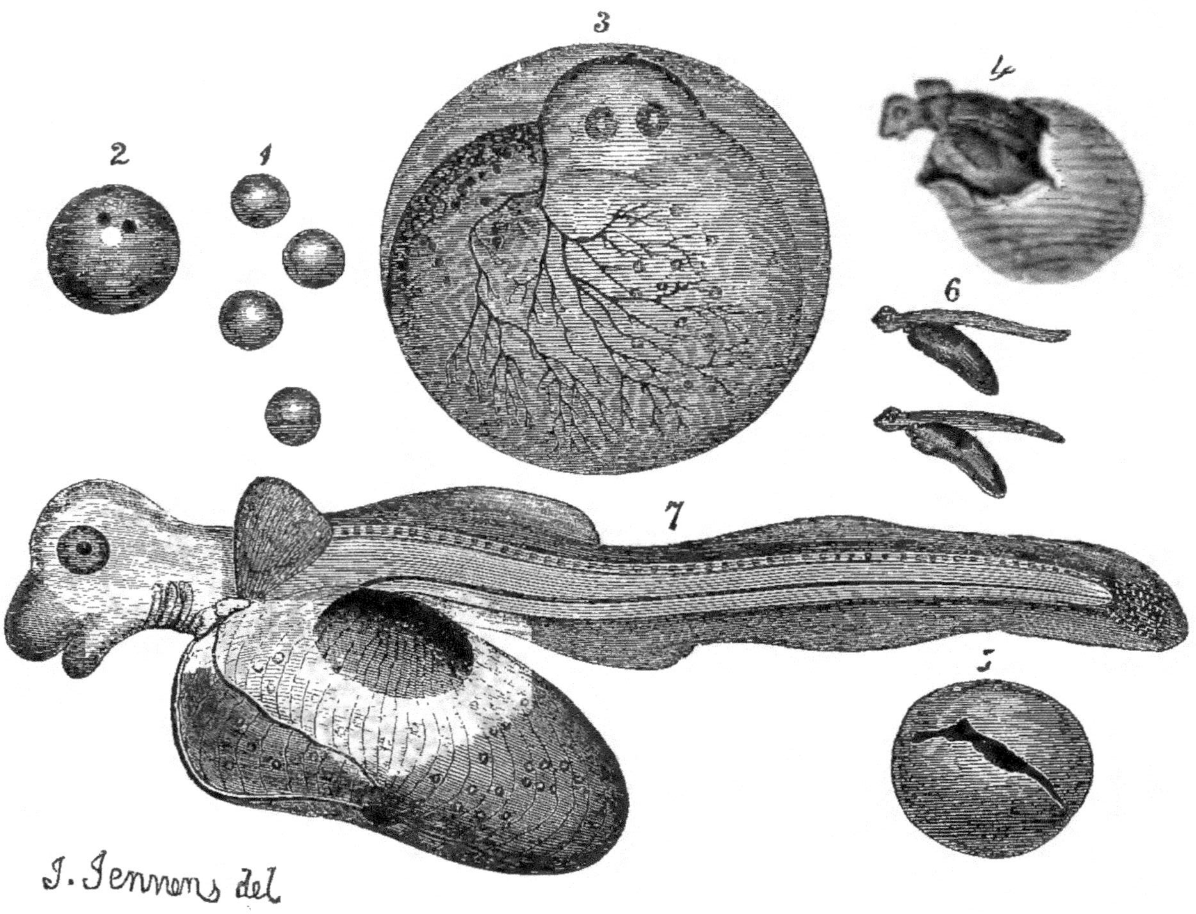

SALMON OVA AND NEWLY HATCHED FISH.

[See page opposite.

DEVELOPMENT OF THE YOUNG SALMON.

No. 1. Egg of salmon, natural size, just taken from the parent fish.

No. 2. The same, with the eyes of the young fish just becoming apparent; this takes place about the thirtieth or thirty-fifth day, according to the temperature.

No. 3. The young fish coiled up in the egg, and just ready to be hatched.

No. 4. The young fish emerging from the shell.

No. 5. The empty egg-shell, showing longitudinal rent made by the young fish.

No. 6. Young salmon about two days old, natural size.

No. 7. The young salmon (about two days old), magnified. The umbilical vesicle, containing the yelk and the oil globules, with blood-vessels ramified on its surface ;—the head—the huge eyes—the badly-developed mouth—the fins—and the thin transparent body, should be observed.

PREFACE.

THE substance of this little book was delivered by myself, in the form of a Lecture, at the Royal Institution, Albemarle Street, on the 17th of April, 1863, and is a record of the observations which I have made during my experiments in Fish Hatching carried on during the winter months. From time to time I have reported progress in the columns of "The Field," and have now, by the permission of the Editor, been enabled to embody my notes in these pages.

I have, however, added much information (though I continue to speak in the first person) derived from the experiences of others, kindly communicated to me; and also from closer subsequent investigation on my own part. I trust that those who read the book will find it useful, and that it will enable them to carry out Fish Hatching on their own account.

I must here record my sincere thanks to Professor Faraday for his kind attention, and also to Professor Tyndall, who was good enough to exhibit the young fish alive under the electric lamp, thereby adding so much to the general interest which I was most pleased to hear was caused among those present on the night of the Lecture.

FRANK T. BUCKLAND.

ATHENÆUM CLUB, PALL MALL,
May, 1863.

CONTENTS.

CHAPTER I.

CHAPTER II.

CHAPTER III.

CHAPTER IV.

FISH HATCHING.

CHAPTER I.

I HAVE been entrusted with the honour of bringing before you, this evening, the important subject of Fish Culture—a trust I feel much pleasure in accepting, and which I hope faithfully and truthfully to be able to discharge. I shall not make any attempts at elocution, but merely endeavour to give plain statements of the results of my own observation, and of other friends interested, both practically and theoretically, in this important matter. This subject as yet has only been considered to be an art, but I trust you will deem, before I have concluded what I have to say, that it is justly worthy of being promoted to, and to take rank among, the true sciences.

The study of the natural products of this earth, whether animate or inanimate, has ever been the aim and object not only of the sons of science, but it has also afforded high intellectual profit and amusement to all classes of intelligent observers.

It has, however, been urged against the study of Natural History that it is not practical, that no actual benefit thereby flows to the public in general. It is, therefore, with the more pleasure that I shall endeavour to show you this evening, by practical demonstration, that in *one* respect at least close observation, followed by close reasoning, has led to the realisation of important practical facts, which promise to be eventually the origin or increase of revenue to private individuals—a source of national wealth, and certainly a great boon to the public in general.

The culture of fish is just now beginning to attract public notice in this highly-favoured and densely-populated island, and it will be my aim to show you both its theory and practice, whereby those who have no opportunity of carrying it out, may reason upon its scientific phenomena: those who have fisheries, ponds, and other waters, may actually develop the theory into practice. But in order that you may rightly understand why fish should be cultivated by artificial means, and why it is so necessary so to do, I would beg to examine—first, the various causes of their scarcity; and, secondly, to point out the means whereby these causes may be avoided, so that your painstaking and care shall be rewarded fourfold.

LAND AND WATER COMPARED.

If you will for a moment observe this wooden globe as I turn it round, you will at once perceive what a vast preponderance the water has over the dry land; in fact, we may fairly say that three-fourths of the whole earth is water. We are for the most part fully cognisant of the inhabitants of the land—we have subjugated those which are serviceable either for food or for labour to our race—but how little do we know of the inhabitants of the water! Man has dominion given him over both land and water. Of the former he has taken every advantage; from the earliest days there have been *agri*-culturists, or land farmers. The human race, however, seem to have entirely forgotten the second item in the double privilege given them; they take no pains to cultivate the largest portion of their earth—the waters. Who ever heard of an *aquæ*culturist or water farmer? We have been asleep—we have had gold nuggets under our noses, and have not stooped to pick them up.

"All that glitters is not gold," nor, again, are seemingly worthless things to be despised as valueless. Tons of fish, worth thousands of pounds, only want a net placed round them, to be converted into bank notes; but they want looking after; they want cultivation. You must not kill your "golden fish" (the "golden goose" may now retire on half-pay), you must not watch the spawning fish-mother to her nest, nor must you permit others to do it—for the sake of her unwholesome carcass (for which the French cook at the Palais Royal will give you a franc or two), destroy her, and at the same time thousands of young fish.

"O, fortunatos nimium, sua si bona norint!" would dear old Virgil have said of the *aquæ*-culturist, if he had known what we now know. You must not, O friend, put your heel upon yon mass of tiny round balls, which, if properly treated, would most assuredly, in about four years, develop themselves into huge silver-coated salmon, and, what is more, will cost you not a penny for food or keep.

This is simply a case of cause and effect. If your gamekeeper *will* put his foot in the nests of the pheasants and partridges, don't whine piteously about having no game. If you keep the coverts quiet in the breeding season, and are rewarded with good sport, you are *not* really lucky, you only reap the reward of foresight and prudence.

Game birds and beasts on land have their coverts—over these strict watch and ward is kept. Over the *water* coverts, forests, and plains, where live and breed the fish, but little labour, if any, is bestowed. You offer a premium, and you issue a *habeas corpu* against hawks, rats, weasels, hedgehogs, and all kinds of so-called vermin destructive to your land game. You allow the *water* vermin to run riot; there are no traps set for *them*; they have their full swing.

Among animals living on land, practical observation will tell us that their rate of increase is, compared to the increase of fish, but very small. In fact, we find it especially recorded that the waters brought forth *abundantly*.

I will proceed to show you that this is the fact.

By way of contrast, we shall first notice that the highest oviparous animals, the birds, produce during the season but a small number of eggs compared to fish: thus, a good barn-door fowl's produce in one year is about 120 eggs. Not trusting to calculations that have had the run of Natural History books for the last fifty years, I have examined the roes of the ordinary fish used for human food, and am enabled to place before you the following table, and also the specimens themselves, to show what an enormous number of eggs are deposited by fish.

But I must tell you how these calculations are made, that you may repeat them for yourselves. I get the mass of the roe from the fishmonger, and these have been kindly and chiefly presented to me by Mr. Grove of Charing Cross, and Mr. Townsend of Agar Street. I make a few cuts in the membrane which contains the roe with a knife, and then plunge them into water, which is at the moment of immersion positively at the boiling point: being composed of albumen, the eggs obey the natural law and coagulate in an instant. I then add a little common salt, and continue to boil the eggs till they all become quite detached from the membrane and swim about in the water loose like marbles; if any adhere to the membrane, they should be gently removed by a soft brush or by shaking in the boiling water. I then, when all the eggs are quite loose, pour off the water and pour the eggs into a meat dish, and dry them *slowly* either in the sun or in the oven, the door of which is left open to prevent their becoming baked into lumps. I then weigh the whole mass of the eggs, and put down the total weight on paper. I then weigh out five grains from the mass, and get them counted over carefully under a magnifying hand-glass on white paper: this is ladies' work.

Having ascertained the number of eggs in five grains, I send off the figures to a young man, Mr. Heap, the son of one of the soldiers in the 2nd Life Guards, who is an excellent arithmetician, which I am *not*, and who returns me the results. By this means, which others can also adopt, I have been enabled to obtain the tables below, and to show you the actual eggs in labelled bottles kept for future reference. Now I have not been Goth enough to destroy a spawning salmon, but experience shows that salmon carry about one thousand eggs to every pound of their weight. The following table, the results of the spawning operations during the last season at the breeding establishments of Stormontfields, will show the actual number in an individual salmon. It has been published in "The Field," in answer to a letter of mine, by Peter of the Pools.

SALMON AND GRILSE NETTED AND SPAWNED AT ALMOND MOUTH FORD, 1862.

Date.	Clean.	Weight in Pounds.	Netted. Salmon.	Netted. Grilse.	Spawned. Salmon.	Spawned. Grilse.	Number of Ova.
November 11	...	...	9	13	...	...	none ripe.
,, 13	1	14	8	39	2	...	10,000
,, 15	...	...	13	14	...	1	4,000
,, 17	...	...	2	7	2 partly	...	18,000
,, 19	1	20	16	30	3	2	40,000
,, 20	1	24	9	17	2	1	22,000
,, 22	...	...	11	14	2	...	20,000
,, 24	...	...	11	19	1	3	24,000
,, 26	...	...	3	5	...	...	none ripe.
,, 28	...	...	6	20	1	9	60,000
December 1	1	14	25	40	3	6	60,000
,, 2	...	...	6	13	2	...	17,000
	4	72	119	231	18	22	275,000

	Weight of Fish.	Total number of Eggs.
Trout*	1 lb.	1,008
Jack	4½ lb.	42,840
Perch	½ lb.	20,592
Roach	¾ lb.	480,480
Smelt	2 ounces	36,652
Lump Fish	2 lb.	116,640
Brill	4 lb.	239,775
Sole	1 lb.	134,466
Herring	½ lb.	19,840
Mackerel	1 lb.	86,120
Turbot	8 lb.	385,200
Cod	20 lb.	4,872,000

These all are the specimens I have been enabled up to this time to examine; I shall

* Trout, like salmon, carry, on an average, 1000 eggs to one pound of their weight; but this rule does not apply to trout under a pound. Again, as regards other fish, the heavier they are the more eggs they carry; therefore I give the weight of the fish I have examined.

feel obliged for further specimens should my readers obtain them.* I must not forget the spawn of the angler-fish (Lophius piscatorius). In Feb., 1862, a fine specimen was sent to me from Brighton. On opening the abdomen I found it three parts filled with a red coloured substance; it was loose, and fell out of the abdomen in the form of a long ribbon: what was my surprise to find that this was all spawn, a mass of genuine eggs! I laid it out, and found upon measuring it that it was no less than *six yards and three quarters* in length; and when spread out broadways presented a flat ribbon seven inches broad, as thickly studded with ova the size of turnip seeds as a rice pudding is with

* Address to "Field" Office, 346, Strand, W.C.

grains of rice. Imagine for a moment the millions, I may say billions of young anglers that would have been produced from this single mother-fish.

The oyster must not be forgotten. T. C. Eyton, Esq., F.L.S., &c., has given us a monograph on its history; he gives the number of young oysters in the shell of the old one at spawning time, and commonly called "the spat," as 1,800,000. The oyster must and *shall* be cultivated in this country. I propose shortly to take the matter in hand. M. Coste and the French pisciculturists have done so much in the way that we ought to be ashamed of ourselves for being all behindhand in this important matter.

ANATOMY OF OVA.

I cannot in this place refrain from a bit of anatomy. You will see in this diagram how the eggs (or ova) are placed in the body of the fish: you may see this fact any morning yourselves when the matutinal herring is placed before you; and you will then understand once for all that the *hard* roe is composed of *the eggs*, whereas the soft roe is the milt of the fish. This diagram of a common trout will show you how these eggs are packed together, and how beautifully they are arranged, reminding one somewhat of figs packed in a box; there is hardly room to place a pin's head between any of them, and they curiously enough resemble a section of a bees' honeycomb.

You may be desirous of knowing how these ova are formed. Here is a preparation from a salmon, which will show you that the ova are thrown off from a long finger-like membrane, one side of which is laminated like the leaves of an opened book; it is in these leaves that the ova are secreted, and you may see some of them still adhering *in sitû.*

I have ascertained for a fact that behind the ova ready to be extruded, say this year, are other ova, as small as pins' heads, which will arrive at maturity next year.

When the ova are ripe they detach themselves from the membrane and lie quite loose in the cavity of the abdomen; they are not, however, I believe, all shed at the same moment, but at various intervals,—so say observers of salmon spawning. They say correctly, as it is not likely that all the ova should become loose at the same moment.

COLOUR OF OVA.

I have observed a curious circumstance as regards the fact that the eggs differ in colour in different trout. At the beginning of this year S. Gurney, Esq., M.P., kindly invited me down to assist in taking the ova from some of his trout, who live a luxurious life in that part of the Wandle which belongs to him. We found the fish quite ripe, and in a few minutes obtained a very ample supply of the most beautiful ova I ever beheld. It was there that I remarked for the first time that the ova of some of the trout were of a splendid coral-red colour; others, on the contrary, were almost as white as peas, yet all good eggs. This depends, it is said, upon whether the trout is a red-fleshed trout or a white-fleshed trout. Again, I found subsequently that the young fish hatched out from the red eggs were much brighter than those hatched out of the yellow eggs: the cause I hope to be able to ascertain when I have a favourable opportunity of examining the flesh of the fish from which the spawn has been taken. This fact as regards the difference of colour in the eggs has been observed by others, for in "The Field" G. A. writes as follows:—

"SIR,—In Mr. Buckland's account of impregnating ova in the Wandle, he speaks of the variety in colour of the ova being attributed by his informant to the colour of the flesh of the parent. Mr. Buckland very rightly says that wants further investigation. I beg to inform him that the same great variety exists in the colour of grayling ova, though the parents in that fish are not red-fleshed. Moreover, the same variety exists in the colour of the yolks of our matutinal eggs, and we don't have red-fleshed hens. The pale and the red fish ova are equally fertile, and the colour does not depend on the age of the parents. These two points I have proved. I cannot believe it to depend on colour of flesh, and therefore attribute it solely to variety in feeding."

Fish ova are exceedingly hard and tough, and very elastic, rebounding from the floor like an india-rubber ball. This is a beautiful provision to prevent them being crushed and otherwise injured by the stones and by the running streams in which they are deposited. The external coating, at least of salmon and trout, is an exceedingly hard, horny, semi-transparent membrane. (See Experiment, p. 29.)

CHAPTER II.

HOW THE FISH DEPOSITS HER SPAWN.

THE word "eggs" necessarily implies the word "nest." Let us now examine the manner in which the fish deposits her eggs, and also the nest—for we may fairly call them nests even though they be only a heap of stones—which the parents provide for them. Birds build with twigs and other vegetable material. The salmon and trout can make no use of these materials, so they deposit them among stones. Other fish, especially sea fish, make use of vegetable material, either as in the case of the stickle-back, building a true nest, or else depositing the eggs upon the fronds and leaves of the plants, some after the manner of insects.

When the fish—I speak now of the salmon and trout—are about to spawn, they set to work and make their nest. They choose, above all places, a shallow gravel bottom, the reason being that there shall be a more rapid flow of water, and hence a greater supply of oxygen to the eggs themselves and also to the young ones when born. The most natural breeding-grounds for the salmon are small, rapid, mountainous streams, deep pools being in the neighbourhood, wherein they can rest and take shelter. They, doubtless, ought to have pools; because, as I said before, a salmon does not deposit her ova at one and the same time, but at intervals. During these intervals she drops back into the pool, and recruits her strength for further operations.

From this simple fact we may learn much as regards the increase of salmon by natural means.* To use the words of that practical man, Mr. Ashworth, in a letter to myself, "We find, and I have seen it, that the smallest streams of pure water are the safest, the most productive, and the very places selected by the parent fish for depositing their ova; and if protected for two months in the winter

* And this is the meaning of the salmon making such vigorous efforts to get up from the sea to the higher waters. Instinct seems to tell them that the young will die in deep water; they therefore make superpiscine efforts to get up cataracts and waterfalls, and attain the shallow brooks. Give them free passage up, and protect them when there, and they will increase and multiply exceedingly.

(December and January), any river may be made productive in which the weirs are made passable by ladders, and in which all natural and insurmountable obstructions, such as rocks, cascades, and falls, are made accessible, and such waters we find are the purest."

The fact of salmon spawning in shallow streams is ably described by Mr. John Miller, the intelligent and active resident superintendent of the Messrs. Ashworth's fisheries, at Galway: —

"GALWAY SALMON FISHERY,
"Weir's House, 10th Jan. 1863.

"I was very much struck yesterday, 9th January, 1863, on walking along a small river called Strawberry Hill. It takes its rise out of a small lake between Tuam and Dunmore, but nearest to the latter, and wends its way for five miles westward, and falls into the Clare river, at Miltown. It is divided into two small branches at the top ; each of these rivulets is about one and a half mile long, and several hundreds of salmon have spawned in each of the rivulets this season. What surprised and interested me most was to see salmon of 5lb. to 7lb. weight sticking so tenaciously in a small stream, and the water so low and so far in the season. I measured the brook in many places with my walking-stick, which is about three feet long, and the average width does not reach the length of my stick. The fish were swimming about in places only two feet wide and one foot deep. They would not leave the place, but swam up and down a dozen yards, and returned to the beds again—no deeper water near them for half a mile on each side. This little river is no exception this season,—there are two streams, equally as small, running through Mr. O'Rork's and Mr. Jackson's lands, at the top of Grange river, where a great many salmon have spawned this season, and where we never observed anything but trout before."

I myself have never had the opportunity of examining a salmon's nest, but I have, to use the schoolboy's expression, "robbed" many a trout's nest. One knows the nest by observing in the bed of the river a hillock, or mound of gravel, about a wheelbarrow full, and a hollow sort of ditch in front of it, as though some one had been scraping it up with his heel. About the beginning of this year I went down to the residence of J. Hibbert, Esq., at Chalfont Park, near Uxbridge, in order to procure trout spawn for his hatching boxes; and as we found that the fish had all spawned, both he and I went into the water to get the eggs from the nest. The mill hatch was put down, so that the stream was much diminished, and we were enabled to scrape the gravel away easily with our hands, like the pictures of monkeys digging up nuts. I was much surprised to find the eggs of the trout at such a considerable depth in the gravel, certainly from one to two feet. They were all about loose in the gravel, reminding one of plums in a pudding. I hollowed out a basin in the nest, and the eggs fell by their own weight into it. When sufficient were collected, I scooped them out with an impromptu net, made of an old soda-water bottle wire and a bit of netting, such as is used by ladies. I cannot understand how the trout manages to get her eggs so deep in the sand. They certainly sink in the water; but one would fancy the current would whip them away in a moment. Again, how is it that they are not often crushed? I have stated above their coats are very elastic; but I had no idea they were so tough. In order to ascertain positively how much direct weight they would bear, in the presence of my brother officers, I tried experiments on the eggs by placing iron stamped weights on individual eggs. I was astonished to find that they were not crushed till I had placed no less than five pounds six ounces on them.

As regards the mode of action and the

relative parts taken by the male and female parent fish in making the nest, in which the female deposits her eggs, I am enabled to give the following important evidence from Mr. C. F. Walsh, of Dundee. He writes to me thus :—

"SIR,—Now, I have seen hundreds of fish in the act of spawning—I have seen as many as thirty brace engaged in the operation at one time, but I never saw the male fish take any part in the work; the *fanning* up of the gravel is all done by the female. I say *fanning*, because I never saw any *boring* of the head into the ground; the female turns on her side, and by strong undulations drives up a cloud of gravel from her tail. How she contrives to remain on the same spot I cannot say; but as they always spawn in a strong current, perhaps she uses only sufficient force to hold against the stream. Stones and gravel are easily moved under water, and therefore the exertion necessary to throw up a bed of gravel is not great. To convince myself of this I put some gravel into a trough of water, and holding a dead fish by the head and on its side, I gently undulated it, and I found the stones were puffed away as if by a gentle breeze of wind. I am aware that in all books on the subject it is said the male makes the ridd, but I am convinced there is no truth in this; the male fish 'wait on,' and their whole spare time appears to be occupied in 'pitching into' every other male fish within sight. They rush on, open-mouthed, and generally turn on their side in striking; and by the time the business is over they are much scratched and scarred. May not the injured state of the head be accounted for by their coming in contact with stones in their headlong assaults?

"I will mention one other thing I have observed. The female fish does *not* first deposit her spawn and then leave it to be impregnated by the male; the male cares nothing for the spawn, except to eat it; his object is to be with the female, for the protection of whom he will fight as long as he is able. The spawning process is carried on in this manner:—The female works away at the ridd, and after she has made a kind of trough she lies in it quite still; the male—who, during the time she is working, is carrying on a constant war—comes up, enters the trough, and assists the female in her efforts to deposit the spawn in the gravel-formed nest which she has heaped up. The male then drops astern. After a short time, the female again throws herself on her side, and fans up the gravel, advancing the trough a little, and covering up the deposited spawn. This operation is repeated till both fish are exhausted. A great quantity of spawn is of course wasted, being eaten by trout and other fish, which are always waiting about for the purpose. The exhaustion of the males is greater than that of the females; they die in numbers; the females do not die. You may pick up a great many exhausted and dead males, but seldom a female.

"C. F. WALSH."

Now, it is well known that at the spawning season the male salmon has an enormous beak, a huge finger-like projection at the top of his lower jaw. I now show you two preparations to demonstrate this fact ; and also a coloured diagram, carefully drawn from nature, by Mr. Jennins.

It is a question as to what this beak really is in structure. Upon making a section I find that it is not bony, but a mass of a purely cartilaginous growth from the bone below. It disappears, moreover, when the salmon is not breeding. I therefore conclude, with Mr. Walsh, that it is simply an offensive and defensive weapon, and is analogous to the horn of the deer.

Anxious to make a closer examination of one of these beaked salmon, I wrote to Mr. Allies, of Foregate Street, Worcester, who kindly sent me a huge salmon which he found dead on the banks of the river Teme. He was 22lb. in weight, and 43 inches in length, and terribly out of condition; if in good condition he would have weighed between 40lb. and 50lb. They called him an "old soldier"—a very fit name,* for many of his scales were of that peculiar dull red which so often adds charms to the rural scenery at that most *delightful* of all places, Aldershot. The *physique*, moreover, of our salmon reminded one of an "old soldier"—a fine old fellow, plucky and brave to the last, but who had served his time, and bearing many scars and wounds upon his person, to say nothing of a great bit of his upper jaw

* A Thames fisherman tells me his father used frequently to find salmon in this condition in the Thames, and they were called "old strikes."

torn away in some fierce conflict with an angler, had summarily retired from the service for want of a Chelsea Hospital.

The cause of his death was doubtless pure exhaustion; there was no actual disease about his body, save and except "bad places" on his scale armour. Whether these were wounds caused by his mining operations in guarding his wife's nest, or simply constitutional, I am unable to state for certain. Mr. George, of Worcester, sent me, moreover, the head of a second spent-salmon, in which the skin is quite worn off the bottom of the lower jaw. The injury in this case I really think, from its appearance—and my idea is confirmed by the opinion of others—was caused by friction against the stones when nest-making.

After I had caused a life-sized water-colour portrait to be made of the "old soldier," I packed him off to the British Museum, where, in a few weeks, he will figure as a beautiful white skeleton, and add much to the interest of Dr. Günther's ichthyological gallery. I asked the doctor if the "old soldier" was big enough for a skeleton; he replied, "He is big enough; did you ever know a big salmon caught but what somebody else had caught a bigger? I shall take him." His skeleton will show what a beautiful bit of water-going architecture there is in a salmon's skeleton.

I have since received a *female* salmon from Mr. Allies, of Worcester, which he found dead after spawning in the Teme. This was a valuable acquisition, for Dr. J. E. Gray requested that she should be presented to the British Museum, and she will shortly be placed in the ichthyological galleries in the form of a skeleton, a fit companion for the "old soldier" I have described above. Dr. Günther and myself made an examination of this fish to ascertain the cause of death. We found that exhaustion was not, as in the male fish, the cause of death. There was actual inflammation and considerable decrease of the left ovary, which was found to be in such a condition as to tell us much of the mode in which the ova are first of all formed and afterwards protruded from the ovary itself. I understand from Mr. Allies that, as a rule, many more male than female fish die after spawning. He says, "I saw five large cock-salmon dead in two miles of water. We have picked up sixteen dead male salmon and but one female." This is a curious fact, rendering it important that those who have the opportunity should examine the dead fish they see in the water, with a view of gaining more knowledge as regards the cause of death in both sexes.

The reason why so many male fish are found dead is, I believe, twofold: first, many die from positive exhaustion; secondly, from wounds inflicted in actual combat. Mr. Samuel Woodcock, of Bury, Lancashire, inclines to the latter opinion, for he writes: "I can explain to Mr. Buckland the reason why so many more male salmon are found dead than females. The males fight desperately, and often kill each other. I have seen them repeatedly lacerated with as many wounds across their backs and sides as a fishmonger inflicts in crimping them. The female has not the perils of war to encounter. In the water these wounds look white, and cause the fish to be distinguished at a great distance. I have frequently discovered a salmon ridd by no other sign than seeing a strip of white, apparently about the length and breadth of two fingers, waving in the stream at right angles to the current. This indicates the wounded warrior, tending his mate, or reposing upon his laurels."

Again, Peter of the Pools writes: "I observe what Mr. Walsh says as to the reason of so many male fish being found dead, and he accounts pretty well for it. Our artificially-spawned fish run no such risks, as the males do not hunt each other, but all are returned carefully to the river, and never a dead one has been found, either male or female, after undergoing the operation. As an instance of safety to the fish, I may mention that a few years ago, a fine male fish of about 20lb. was used for spawning purposes at Stormontfields. A mark was put on him by means of a piece of copper wire, and two years afterwards he was got when nearly 30lb. weight on the same ford and at the same season; and, after doing duty again was returned to the river hale and strong, but was not traced afterwards."

CHAPTER III.

ENEMIES OF OVA.

Now, supposing the nest to be made, and the ova deposited therein, how many of them will ever come to life, or grow up to be fish fit for human food? As in the case of Virgil's bees, we hear with sorrow, "Tum varia illudunt pestes." What a catalogue of these "pests of the water" to the new-born, tender, and helpless little salmon, can we enumerate! Let us examine these in detail.

First, accidents at the time of spawning. Many of the eggs do not get properly impregnated at the time of spawning, or not being caught by the gravel, are washed away constantly by the stream. Then down come the floods and overwhelm the nests with mud and rubbish, or else sweep them bodily away, level to the bed of the river. Here is a case in point: Mr. Buist writes in "The Field," March, 1863, "From eighteen salmon and twenty-two grilse we had filled our breeding-boxes with 275,000 ova. Immediately *after* our ponds were filled the rivers came out in great floods, which dispersed the salmon, and, it is feared, that as these floods continue till the end of December, the fine appearance of fish would come to little account when left to all the contingencies of spawning in the rivers. The 310 fish not spawned would all be ripe within ten days, so that from those left to *their natural course* there would not have been so many fecundated eggs from the 310 as we have in the breeding-boxes from the forty fish. All these fish were caught on one ford where the Almond joins the Tay."

Then again, we have the reverse of floods —we have droughts; and the nests made when the water is high become bare and exposed to the air when the water goes down; either the eggs die from this cause, or else the young when hatched out, having no water, "refuse to exist."

I have seen a shallow ditch leading out of Ruislip Reservoir one mass of dead fry of roach, dace, and jack, the water having been let out for the canal.

Nor must we forget mill-wheels. Here is

evidence from a writer in "The Field":—
"On one of the principal breeding streams that supplies the Shannon, within the last few years a new tail race was made at the Ballyartellagh mill, on the Nenagh river, and the fish are able, in their endeavours to get up stream, to pass a certain distance under the wheel, when they are struck on the head or back of the head by it, and either killed or so much injured that they drop down stream and die. On one occasion, after a small summer flood, when but few fish were running, I saw *thirteen* picked up; and if this takes place at that time of year, what must be the destruction when the large run of spawning fish takes place in the autumn? It is already provided that there shall be guards both above and below, but the old

cry of interfering with the milling powers has made it a dead letter." The same thing happens to trout. I picked one up at Carshalton, killed by a decided scalp wound from a mill-wheel.

Second, fish eat the eggs, and these not only minor fish but trout, who wait below the nest and scramble for the eggs, like boys scrambling for coppers; nor am I certain but that the trout will actually go and rout for what eggs they can manage to pick up *out* of the nest, for Andrew, the keeper at Hampton, has seen them with their noses grubbing in the nests, and their tails projecting out of the water, like so many sharks' fins out at sea. I have myself taken trout eggs from a trout's mouth, and so have other observers, for Mr. Woodcock writes as follows:—"On December 9th, whilst the keepers were netting the river Dunlop, for salmon for my use, I examined a small stream on the bog, noted for the quantity of trout which breed in it. We took a number of male fish—sea-trout and river-trout—before we caught a female. Observing a number of ova in the trough in which I deposited them for a temporary purpose, I was led to inspect their throats, and every male fish I examined except one had ova in its maw. I had a still stranger account from a friend of mine, who was getting a stock of breeding-trout for the Ribble. He had taken seven pair of trout, and had placed them, with Ramsbottom's sanction, in a small pool for safety, until the time for manipulating had arrived. When these fish came to be examined, it was found that all the females, except one, had entirely got rid of their ova, and the seventh partly so, and that every fish, male and female, except the one which had only partially spawned, was absolutely gorged with ova.

"I never remember to have seen either of these incidents recorded before; and they are both capable of being verified by ample testimony. What wonder that trout should be scarce when both mother and father devour the ova!"

Again, Mr. Ashworth tells me that he has taken no less than 500 peas (fish eggs) from the maw of one trout. He placed these by themselves in a hatching-box, and most of them in due time produced young fish. Salmon, too, will eat their own eggs, and we used formerly to see salmon ova, preserved in salt, sold at the fishing-tackle shops for bait. This mode of fishing is so deadly that it is now made illegal.

Then we have water insects innumerable. The common water shrimp, for instance, of which I now show specimens, finds out the nests, and treats the eggs with as much mercy as rats do the grain in a wheat stack. These water shrimps will get into hatching-boxes, and if ever we choose an animal to lead a forlorn hope into a fortress, let it be the water shrimp ; if he cannot get in himself through the perforated wire, he sends in the junior members of his family, who, sharing the fate of Horace's weasel, grow so fat and well that they cannot get out again.

Mr. Godfrey, the proprietor of Thorney Broad Fishery, near Uxbridge, tells me that at the spawning time the roach actually covers the weeds near his weir; the water shrimps and other insects come down upon them like the hop dogs upon the hops in Kent, and in a very short time clear them almost entirely away. It is a question whether the caddis worm attacks eggs or not. I rather think not, but I am not yet certain.*

Besides the water shrimp we have the larva of the May-fly (specimen exhibited), a sort of just retribution against the fish, who will eat them when they turn into May-flies. These formidable creatures do

* See in Appendix an account of some curious experiments on the caddis, by Mr. Smee.

an immensity of harm. They fasten on the egg, pierce them with their sharp nippers, and they turn white and dead in an instant. The Messrs. Ashworth, of Galway, report that, in one year they deposited 70,000 salmon ova in a small pure stream adjoining a plantation of fir-trees, and these ova they found to be entirely destroyed by the larva of the May-fly. More evidence on this point can be found in "Life in Normandy."

The larva of the dragon-fly is also a destructive pest of the waters, and has been justly called the river tiger. I show specimens of the river tiger, which Mr. Allies caught in a salmon's nest in the river Teme, in Worcestershire.

There are other insects which eat the

spawn besides those above mentioned. Observers, observe for yourselves!

4th. *Human Poachers.*—At the time of spawning, the salmon or trout—usually as wild as a fox—becomes as tame as a barn-door fowl, and any little boy walking by the side of the stream can kill them with a stick,—become the easy prey of the poachers, and millions of their eggs are destroyed which would otherwise have been deposited. Tons weight are at this time captured and sent to Paris; why they do not kill the people who eat them there I know not. Anyhow, these fish are poisonous to Englishmen. Mr. Ashworth's head bailiff knows this from practical experience. He once ate a portion of one, and in consequence was made so ill that he was confined to his bed for two days, and he was a strong, powerful, healthy man.

I now show you a magnificent clean-run fish, weighing between 30 and 40 pounds: that is a salmon for the Englishman. That—(pointing to the kelt)—is "*vrai saumon écossais*" of the Palais Royal cooks.

These wretched poisonous fish are exported to France under all possible disguises—sometimes packed in baskets as game, with the feet and tails of game birds and beasts protruding from the baskets, sometimes even as fruit-trees. The British Fisheries Preservation Association have taken the matter up in a most praiseworthy manner, and are doing their best, by appeals and representations to Government authorities, both in England and France, to stop this destructive export of spawning fish. We must all wish them success in the effort.

It may have struck my readers that I have not mentioned, among the pests of the fisheries, the water-ouzel and the dab-chick. I do this advisedly, as I have inquired carefully into the matter, and now publish, by permission of the Editor, the correspondence, and the results which have been obtained through the medium of the columns of "The Field."

"I enclose a water-ouzel, shot in the very act of poaching (?) on a spawning ford. If Mr. Buckland cannot find traces of roe in its stomach, even making all allowance for rapid digestion, I shall certainly spare the lively, innocent little fellow in future.—RIFLEMAN (Sutherland, Jan. 17)."

"[I have, as 'Rifleman' wished, made a most careful examination of the bird, from the stomach downwards. I was pleased to find the gizzard (which is by no means very muscular) quite full. I placed it in a vessel of clean water, divided it in half, and emptied out the contents, the whole of which I passed in detail under the object-glass of a microscope. I could not find the least trace of fish ova; I looked especially for the horny egg-cases, for these would be the most likely portions of the egg to escape digestion, but I could not find any appearance whatever of them. The contents of the gizzard consisted entirely of the hard external cases of water insects, portions of the legs with the hooks attached, and broken fragments of other portions of their bodies, intermixed with some vegetable structure, and several small fragments of gravel and transparent quartz. If 'Rifleman' should see another water-ouzel on the spawning-beds, I should much like him to get it and send it to me, that I may repeat the examination. Water insects are attracted in large numbers to fish ova, and the bird I have examined evidently knew this fact.—F. T. BUCKLAND.]"

"The notice in your paper of last Saturday, that one of these birds had been sent to Mr. Buckland for examination, caused me to look over my notes on this subject, made in the spawning season 1856-7. Up to that period I, in common with other preservers of salmon and trout, took it for granted that, because this bird is so constant a visitor on the salmon, while that fish is spawning, it is so solely for the purpose of feeding upon the ova, and, in consequence, thinking I was getting rid of an enemy, I took great pains to destroy as many as possible. Amongst those I killed, twenty fell to my gun just as they emerged from spawning-beds, every one of which I at once opened from bill to gizzard. On examination both before and after washing, with the naked eye and under the microscope, I could not in one single instance discover a trace of ova, neither of case of ova, nor of the oleaginous matter which forms the contents of the case; instead of this, I found the stomach full of the larvæ of flies, whole and in fragments, and always more or less of fine sand. About this date I heard of the destruction of ova in the boxes at Stormontfield by the larvæ of the stone-fly, and it immediately occurred to me that I was destroying a most efficient assistant, and that the water-ouzel was one amongst the many exquisite links constantly presenting themselves to the student of the natural history of this valuable fish. During the formation of the spawning-bed, the salmon turns over gravel, in the interstices of which lie the larvæ of aquatic flies, to which the water-ouzel is debarred access until so turned over by the salmon ; and the more frequent the visits of this useful bird to the newly-turned gravel, the freer will the spawning-bed be from these hurtful insects. This opinion subsequent experience has confirmed, and preservers of salmon will act wisely to protect, as a most able assistant, the falsely-accused water ouzel.—J. H. Horsfall."

"Allow me to add my testimony to that of Mr. Horsfall. Some years ago, when a discussion was rife on this question, I caused a dozen of these birds to be shot during the breeding-season, and on the breeding streams. On examining their food, I could find nothing but sand and water insects, and their remains—not a trace of ova of any kind. I believe the water-ouzel to be entirely innocent.—SAMUEL WOODCOCK (Bury, Lancashire, Jan. 31)."

"As I noticed some remarks on the subject of the water-ouzel and fish ova, I procured one of these birds, which was shot in the act of feeding; and having dissected the stomach and gizzard, found the inclosed, which I send for Mr. Buckland's inspection. It consists, apparently, of the remains of insects ; but, if Mr. Buckland will put it in water and examine it closely, he will find a small spine (?) of a fish.—H. E. Fox (Rydal, Jan. 20)."

["I have examined the contents of this bird's gizzard, and, as in the former case, can find nothing but a mass of the horny cases, legs, hooks, &c., of water insects, and not a trace of fish ova. I could not, unfortunately, find the spine mentioned by Mr. Fox. In the last specimen I examined, there were several spine-like bodies, which, however, were forms of *infusoria*. From the evidence now before us, I think we can hardly help the conclusion that the water-ouzel goes to the spawning-beds, not to eat the spawn, but to eat the insects that destroy the spawn, and which are, as pisciculturists well know, attracted by it. It is, moreover an illogical conclusion, that, because a bird is seen on the spawning-beds, it *therefore* eats the spawn. We want a third premise in the syllogism. The poor water-ouzel may, therefore, after all, be the friend, not the enemy, of the proprietors of fisheries.—F. B."]

"Having seen a water-ouzel visiting my hatching ponds, I shot it, and subsequently I killed three more near a natural spawning-bed. After dissecting these birds I found one ovum just devoured, but as it was not of the healthy pink colour, but was white, I suppose that the ouzel had picked it out, not for the sake of the roe, but for some insect which at the time was feeding upon the egg. The gizzards contained nothing besides remnants of insects. The bill of the ouzel not being formed for shovelling in large objects, such as salmon roe, but for picking such small things as insects, I should say that they are an instrument in the hands of an all-wise Providence, for removing insects feeding upon the ova, and at all events such an insignificant means could not have been chosen for the purpose of neutralising the too great increase of salmon. I think it wisest for man not to interfere in the management, and to spare my lively little friend the water-ouzel. — GOTHENBURGER, February 14."

At a scientific meeting of the Zoological Society, in February, 1863, among other points that I brought foward for discussion was the various causes of the destruction of the ova in their natural state. I quoted the results, as regards the water-ouzel, already obtained by myself and other gentlemen (especially the gentleman whose letter I now have by me), and which have been lately published in "The Field," all the evidence of the witnesses going to prove that the contents of the water-ouzel's gizzard were *not* ova, but the remains of water insects.

John Gould, Esq., F.R.S., the highest European authority on all relating to birds, &c., then put into my hands the last number of his magnificent work, "The Birds of Great Britain," and requested me to read aloud to the meeting the following:—

"Among fishermen the water-ouzel has a bad character, from their belief that it feeds upon the ova of the trout and salmon; hence in some parts of Scotland it is destroyed by every device; but the charge, in my opinion, has not been established, nor have I any reason, after taking considerable pains to investigate the subject, to believe that it is just. During my visit, in November, 1859, to Penwyre, the seat of Colonel Watkyns, on the river Usk, the water-ouzels were very plentiful, and his keeper informed me that they were then feeding on the recently-deposited roe of the trout and salmon. By the Colonel's desire, five specimens were shot for the purpose of ascertaining by dissection the truth of this assertion, but I found no trace whatever of spawn in either of them. Their hard gizzards were entirely filled with larvæ of *Phryganea* and the water beetle (*Hydrophilus*). One of them had a small bull-head (*Cottus Gobio*) in its throat, which the bird had doubtless taken from under a stone. I suspect that insects and their larvæ, with small-shelled mollusks, constitute their principal food; and it may be that their labours in this way are rather beneficial than otherwise; for as many aquatic insects will attack the ova and fry, their destruction must be an advantage. I believe, indeed, that birds generally, nay always, do good rather than harm in the check they give to the undue extension of insect-life; and it is not a little interesting to observe how their varied forms are adapted to this particular end. There is no element, and scarcely a situation, in which insects can live, that is out of the reach of their more powerful enemies the birds."

The water-ouzel having, therefore, been fairly put on his trial, the verdict first arrived at by the gentlemen assembled was "Not proven." A distinguished ornithologist present considered this was not sufficiently strong; the jury thereupon reconsidered their decision, and ultimately returned their verdict thus: "Water-ouzel *fully acquitted* of the charges of eating fish spawn." I hope the readers of this will also agree in this opinion.

Besides the water-ouzel, the dabchick has been accused of eating the spawn. I have examined the contents of the gizzards of two of these, that *were shot in the spawning-beds*, and sent to me to report upon. The first specimen contained *insect* remains hardly digested at all; in the second the contents of the stomach were more comminuted. I therefore sent them to a microscopic friend, who reports as follows *:—"I have carefully examined the remains of the bird's food, but cannot find any signs of fish ova having formed part of his diet. The matters you have sent are entirely insect, and consist of legs, wing cases, and a caddis-worm case."

There are now, I should mention, two living dabchicks in the aquarium house at the Zoological Gardens; and, though such a common bird, Mr. Bartlett has hitherto had great difficulty in procuring living specimens. I went into the water and took out of a net with my own hands the female, when we were catching trout to take the ova for hatching purposes. The little creature went with a terrible bang into the net, swimming under water, and we thought we had got a very

* "The Field," March, 1862.

large trout. I took her carefully out, and gave her to Mr. Bartlett, who has since got a mate for her. We have learned a fact from these two pretty birds. There are a great number of small fish in their quarters at the Zoological, and they eat an enormous number of them, diving after and pursuing them with arrow-like velocity. If, therefore, they do *not* devour the spawn of trout, they will the young fish.

We have acquitted the water-ouzel and dabchick of eating the ova, but now I bring the charge against the common house (not water) rat, for Froude—the intelligent keeper to Mr. S. Gurney, M.P.—has written to me to tell me, that these rascals had made a run and got into the house where the ova were deposited, and actually devoured several of them from off the glass rods. They must have got into the water to get at them.

I want, moreover, information about the water-shrew. I hear that this little fellow eats the ova ; his teeth are insectivorous, but still he may eat fish-eggs. The accusation, anyhow, has been brought against him, and I should much like to inquire into the matter.

There are birds who are most destructive to spawn, and common ducks lead the van of these feathered poachers. I saw a lot the other day hard at work on a spawning-bed, as I was looking over the bridge at Romsey, and watching the trout in Lord Palmerston's beautiful fisheries. Readers, if you want fish, drive off the ducks ; you cannot have both. Again, the swans are *most* destructive ; though ornamental, they are *more* than useless, particularly in ponds and in the river Thames, where they do incalculable mischief to the fisheries, and slay their millions, gobbling up the newly-laid spawn with their long beaks and spoon-like bills. In 1861, I was deputed to report, with the late lamented Mr. Arthur Smith, upon this point, and we sent in a report to the British Fisheries Preservation Association, recording our actual observations of these poachers, taken when they were at work, for which purpose we made a voyage on the Thames, near Windsor. I myself, therefore, am fully convinced of the immensity of harm they do to the Thames, but I prefer calling other witnesses as well, for the subject has been well ventilated in "The Field," and every year it turns up again about the end of April or beginning of May.

Thus, in May, 1861, Mr. Francis Francis, the Angling Editor, a highly experienced and good observer, writes—"I happened to meet Milbourne, the water-bailiff, while fishing up the river a day or two since, and I asked him what he thought of the swans eating the spawn? He said, 'Lord bless you, sir; they not only *eat* it, but they eat *nearly all of it.* At this very time there has been as fine a lot of jack as ever I saw spawning in Walton Reach. They spawned up the ditches and cuts, and as soon as they spawned the swans would go up the ditches after them and eat it all up; and you could not drive them away. Some people, who don't know anything about it, won't believe it. I called Mr. Wheatley, of Walton, out a few days ago. He wouldn't believe it, and I showed him the swans gobbling the perch spawn down off the bows by quarts. 'What d'ye say to that now?' says I. 'I wouldn't have believed it,' says he. And no one would who didn't see it, sir. Last year they ordered the breeding of swans to be stopped. This year they have continued it again. The number of swans already between Walton and Staines is beyond belief. They swarms there; and if they're to be allowed to breed, we shall have such a mess of swans that the river will be regularly smothered with them. Suppose they don't know where nor how to find the spawn? Gammon! Don't a donkey know where to look for thistles, and don't I know where beefsteaks grow?'

"Any gentleman who doubts the mischief the swans do, can now have ocular demonstration, as they are just finishing off the perch and jack spawn, and will be ready in a few days for the roach, chub, and barbel. I made a little calculation as to the quantity of fish they keep from the river every year, and at the very lowest computation that can be made, it amounts to one hundred millions. At a more reasonable and probable calculation, it is possibly nearer a thousand millions. No wonder sport is indifferent—no wonder the roach and dace are disappearing!"

He is followed by Greville F. thus: "An owner of a piece of once-excellent and well-stocked water, near here (Kintbury on the Kennett, near Admiral Dundas's), chuckled mightily over the gift of three brace of swans, which served two years to decorate his domain. His stock of fish, however, dwindled and dwindled away, and men were set at night to watch for poachers who never came. About the middle of last year, I bethought me of your remark, 'that he had taken to the bosom of his waters' a set of downy rascals who would not leave the weight of a scale therein.' I told him of this; he had one of their craws examined; evidence of their piscatorial pursuits was there in plenty. The other five underwent a similar examination, and they were plucked. The water is gradually assuming its old character, but it will require at least two or three years, and the absence of all swans, to restore it to what it was. The worthy landlord of the angling hostelrie at Weybridge, the elder Harris,. writes, 'there never was no manner of doubt about the dreadful mischief the swans do. They eats up the spawn of every kind of fish until they have filled their bags, and then on to shore they goes, to sleep off their tuck-out, and then at it again.' What is to be done! Another spawning season has gone over, and still the devastation remains in fuller force than ever. Cannot some movement be organised that shall have for its object the protection of the next year's fecundation?"

Again, we read in "The Field," of about the same date, the following:—"The old adage of Marlborough that 'we should never under-rate an enemy,' applies to swans as well as men. I, therefore, hasten to modify, in some measure, the statement I have made, that these creatures may be readily kept off the spawning-beds, and that a lad placed upon each of such localities during the short period of 'nature's process' would serve this purpose. This, I now regret to be compelled to say, would be wholly inefficient. Let those who think otherwise repair forthwith to Penton Hook (by-the-by, what has this beautiful locality done to the makers of maps, that it should be left entirely out of nineteen out of twenty of the charts of the Thames?), and he will find his work already cut out for him. The grayling are now spawning there, and can be seen by any one approaching them quietly in a boat, upon the side of the Hook, which empties itself into the main river; and there likewise is a flock of swans (literally the debit for the credit) totalling up the whole, and leaving no balance behind. The water-bailiff at Laleham has done his best to drive them off, and although he may succeed in getting them down a mile or two, they are back again directly his back is turned, with perhaps three or four more of their kind, politely (it may be) invited to the feast, or attracted, not unlikely, by the spawn around their gourmandising bills. I, therefore, infer that unless powers be given to the bailiffs to use more than gentle means, the London City Companies must lie under the imputation that they are permitting these Dandos of spawn to eat and waste that which in common honesty they cannot but conscientiously acknowledge to be the property of others.—GREVILLE F."

"I think I can bear testimony to swans

being more destructive to the spawn of fish on the Thames than has yet been mentioned. I was fishing from a coracle moored at the mouth of the river that debouches into the Thames by Egham Weir, when a swan came up the river, crowding all sail, in great wrath, to drive me out of his dominions. He came on until he was within the length of my rod, which I dropped to lay hold of the paddle, as he seemed bent on capsizing my craft with his wing. Suddenly, however, he turned an eye on the water, and, poking his head and neck down, he rushed several yards, bringing up a bleak of the largest size in his mouth, which he turned and swallowed, head first, as quick as a heron could do. Thus his wrath was appeased; but I heartily wished for an air-cane gun, when I certainly would have stopped his further poachings—maugre the £5 penalty.—PERIPLECTOMENES."

"A friend informed me, last week, that he was walking by a pond in which was a brace of swans. The large carp were spawning and were rolling over the water-weed like pigs, and he assured me that the swans actually lay beside the carp, and eat the spawn as it came from them, and a gentleman who lives close to the pond told him that he had constantly seen them doing it. In another pond I know of, some years ago, there was a quantity of small fry (young carp and tench) always in the pond. A pair of swans were put on, and now there are a few fish of two and three pounds weight, but nothing smaller, and very few of them; as the young stock is killed every year by the swans, of course there is none hatched to replace the fish that are caught.—FRANCIS FRANCIS."

Besides the above, I have letters innumerable on the same point, all agreeing that the swans should be considerably thinned.

The Hon. Spencer Ponsonby tells me that the swans, in consequence of these and other representations, were diminished in quantity, but they sadly want looking after again. Never did I feel so much pleased as when, in the autumn of last year, I saw a boat-load of these feathered poachers floating down the river, each one in a basket all to himself, the result of a swan-hopping expedition.* The swans belong, I believe,

* A great many of these swans were sent to Australia, and I hope they may be soon joined by their relatives.

to the Woods and Forests and the Dyers' and Vintners' Companies.

We have seen now, therefore, what some of the causes of destruction of fish eggs are. I say nothing of the desolating causes after they are grown up into fish.

The results are—we will take the case of the king of fishes, the salmon—that, according to given data and accurate calculations of the returns of fisheries made by Messrs. Ashworth and Buist, only *one salmon's egg out of every thousand deposited by the parent fish ever becomes a fish fit for human food.* Other fish, both fresh and salt water, suffer in proportion, or we should not have such long prices to pay for turbot, soles, and other first-class fish at the fishmonger's.

CHAPTER IV.

ON THE PROTECTION OF THE EGGS, AND HATCHING THEM BY ARTIFICIAL MEANS.

Thus, then, Gentlemen and Ladies, I have endeavoured to demonstrate to you the immense difficulties which surround on all sides the eggs of salmon, trout, and other fish, when deposited in their natural state by the parent fish. I wish now to show you how these difficulties are to be obviated, and how human care can be brought to bear upon the eggs of these really valuable animals.

Instead, therefore, of allowing the ova to be deposited in the natural nest, we catch the fish in a net, we take the eggs from her,* we treat them in the manner which was first discovered by two poor fishermen (honour to their memory) and afterwards developed by M. Coste, professor of embryology at Paris, and we place them in an artificial nest, such as I will endeavour to explain to you.

In the first place, you must provide an artificial nest, and, in the second, an artificial mother. Now the former consists of gravel placed in a narrow box, either of wood, earthenware, or zinc ; the latter consists of a stream of shallow water, which shall be running day and night.

For hatching on a large scale I recommend you to procure boxes such as this—a model of

* The manner of doing this is fully detailed at the end of the book, for the benefit of those who wish to perform the operation.

those used by Mr. Ashworth. It is made of elm, oak, or deal, and is six feet long, eight inches deep, twelve inches wide, an enlarged mignonette box in fact. You must recollect the two requisites—a running stream and shallow water. You must fix the box according to your locality. You can place it either in a narrow, fast-running ditch which you know will never fail you, or, better still, place it near a spring where you can regulate the flow of water by means of hatches, large or small. You must guard both the entrance and the exit of the box with a bit of perforated zinc, the holes of which must be sufficiently large not to obstruct the current of water; and you should also have a plate of perforated zinc fixed in any convenient place, a foot or two above the box, to stop the scum, &c., of the water. Above this may be placed an extra sentry, viz., a new birch broom; saw off the handle close to the twigs, and fix it with the loose ends of the twigs pointing up stream. These twigs will catch the weeds and other mess that come down with the water. The cleaner the water you pass into the eggs the better for them.

You should have wire covers, which can be padlocked to the boxes, to keep out the shrew mice and rats, and the fingers of meddling boys; and you should have boards ready to place over these to keep out the light during the incubation of the ova.

These boxes may be multiplied *ad infinitum*, so that the water that passes through No. 1

should fall into No. 2, and so on, like water falling down (only at the ends) from one step of a staircase on to the step below it. The box should be a little inclined to favour the flow of water, and the water should have a fall from the end of one box into the head of another of a few inches. You must take care so to level and arrange the boxes as that, should the stream from above fail, *some* water should always be left to cover the eggs. If you have not convenience for placing the boxes in a parallel row, you can place them side by side, at right angles to the stream whence the water is derived, having a hatchway for each.

Your boxes being all ready for putting down into the stream, get some gravel, river gravel will not do, but dig it out of a gravel pit, sift it through a sieve—the meshes of which are half an inch—and when you have enough sifted, *boil it* for an hour or so in a copper till it is quite clean. The boiling destroys the sporules of the vegetation, and also the eggs of the minor water beasts that eat the spawn. Then get the mason or the carpenter to fix the boxes in the stream, or better do it yourself; get the levels right by means of bricks, wedges of wood, &c., and then wheel down the gravel to the place; then, with a spade, carefully deposit in the boxes your boiled half-inch sized gravel, to the depth of about two or more inches. You must then place a layer of about one inch in thickness, or one and a half, of gravel stones —take them as they come—each stone being about the size of a walnut. The reason of this stratification is that the young fish, being hatched under the big stones, shall not get down much below this level, being stopped by the half-inch gravel. Set your stream going for a few hours, and see that it works properly, being always about two or three inches in depth, and flowing perpetually.

Now then you are ready for the eggs. When you have got them, carefully distribute them with a spoon among the big stones under which they will naturally roll, and leave them alone. The stream should be gentle and continuous, but not fast enough to bother the eggs.

Should the reader not understand this, let him go down to Hampton, near Hampton Court, and Mr. Ponder will show him his boxes at work, and he will see the whole thing in a moment.*

With all your precautions for keeping the stream clear, you will find a deposit settle on the eggs, and this to a greater or less extent. To avoid this, *keep them dark;* put boards over the tops of the boxes, and, if you please, get some common roofing slates, and place these on your walnut-sized stones, taking care that the water shall flow freely under them. You will find the slates will catch the deposit which falls from above downwards, and you can easily take them out and wash them when dirty. It is, in my opinion, a mistake, to actually bury the eggs in gravel; the slates and the walnut-

* If Mr. Ponder is not at home, ask at the Red Lion Hotel for the keys, and the keeper, Andrew, will go with you.

sized stones are sufficient protection. All you want is darkness, which is unfavourable to vegetation, and your boards and your slates will do all this.

There is no objection to your lifting up the stones every now and then, to see that the eggs are all right, and to pick out the dead ones, *i.e.*, those that are turned white, either with a forceps or a glass tube of the right diameter, to catch the egg.* You may, too, brush the eggs with a soft camel-hair brush, but do it gently—very gently—as moving them disturbs the vivification of the young fish that is going on inside. When the egg is developed, as will be explained hereafter,

* Put your finger on the top of the tube, pass it down to the egg you wish to catch, take your finger off, and the egg will mount instantly into the tube.

there will be no danger whatever in moving them.

So much, therefore, for the *out-door* apparatus, which, by the way, should not be too far from the dwelling-house, or it will be neglected. It will work well if properly managed, and operations are required on a large scale; but for ordinary experiment I far prefer the in-door apparatus; because this can be fixed up in a green-house, or other convenient place, and can be watched with greater ease without exposure of the observer to the cold during the winter months, during which the process of hatching will be going on.

Now the in-door apparatus consists of a series of boxes, about the size of mignonette boxes, or even smaller; those used by Mr.

Smee are 20 inches long, 4½ deep, and 6 wide, which can be placed one above the other, so that the water can fall either by means of lips over the sides, or over the ends, like my boxes in the "Field" Office. These boxes may be made either of zinc or earthenware.* The water can be caused to flow from a cistern, and will run down through as many boxes as you please to place one above the other, either side to side, or else end to end. These boxes must contain either a series of glass rods, upon which the eggs can sit, and which is a neat and clean way of hatching them, or can be filled with the *boiled* half-inch gravel, so that two inches of

* By next September or October I shall be able to tell the reader where these may be procured, or any how can give him a model.

water can be always running over them; regulate your stream by means of stop-cocks, and find a place for the waste water to run. The water would be all the better for being filtered. This is not absolutely necessary, if it is naturally pretty pure, but it is certainly advisable. Filter it through charcoal, gravel, sand, or any other simple and commodious material. The *same* water, if clean, may be used over and over again; but fresh water is, of course, preferable.

If the reader does not understand this, let him call at the "Field" Office, 346, Strand, and see my apparatus at work, or let him pay Mr. Ponder a visit; this gentleman (or in his absence his keeper) will be pleased to allow visitors to examine the boxes by means of which he has met with such great success in fish hatching.

All things ready, place your ova either on the glass rods or on the gravel; have a bit of board ready, fitting the tops of the boxes accurately, to keep out all the light (which is so favourable to vegetation), and look at the eggs every morning, to see how they are getting on. You should also support, by means of stones or pegs fixed into the gravel, bits of roofing slates over the eggs, to prevent the deposit, after the manner suggested for the out-of-door boxes.

You will, of course, find some of the eggs die. Even the most attentive human nurse will lose some of the eggs, and you will know these in a moment. The egg, instead of being a bright pink and fresh colour, turns to an opaque, or pale white colour; this is a sure sign that it is dead. Remove it instantly, for it will most assuredly contaminate all its neighbours. They will adhere to it as if fastened by strong glue, and in a short time they also will die. A curious fungus, too, you will see, will spring up upon these dead eggs, and if you place one by itself in a bottle, you will see the fungus growing up from it on all sides, like the hair of a doll electrified in the electrifying machine.

Do not disturb the eggs more than you can possibly help. If the deposit is very great, attend to your filter; carefully increase the stream of water, and in time you will be rewarded by observing that the egg is vivified. You will know this by observing two black specks appear in the egg, which are the eyes of the future fish, and you will also see a faint line running around nearly three-quarters of the egg, the body of the future salmon or trout. When you see this, congratulate yourself the egg is alive, and will probably hatch out all right.*

The time of the eye appearing, and of the young fish hatching out, depends entirely upon the temperature.

It is a most curious thing to observe how greatly temperature affects the development of the ova into the young fish, and I look upon this, not only as a most interesting physiological phenomenon, but also as a beautiful provision of nature, that the young

* See drawing.

fish should not be hatched out *too soon,* too early in the year, and acquire its mature growth before the food on which it subsists is to be found, but that they should both be produced simultaneously. Keep therefore your temperature low, or you will hatch your fish out too early in the season. This is one of the first results I obtained. Thus "The Field" window began to hatch on the 16th of January, at the temperature of 52° to 55°. The Zoological fish did not begin to hatch till Jan. 21, the temperature being from 48° to 50°. The temperature made all this difference; but mark again another and most important difference. The fish which take the longest time to hatch are always the strongest fish of the two; a fact which agrees with Mr. Ponder's observations at his green-house apparatus at Hampton.

Mr. Bartlett has informed me that he had hatched salmon ova in the short space of thirty days from the time of impregnation; and he has given me notes of observations which he published at the time. Curiously enough, Mr. Ponder has arrived at somewhat similar results with trout ova at Hampton, last year.

This is the experience at Stormontfields as regards temperature, as sent me by Mr. Buist.

"Of the 275,000 ova in our boxes, the whole are now (March, 1863) quick and bursting into life, a great many of them are already hatched, and the others are very healthy, and the young fish may clearly be seen in them, and are bursting the shell daily. In consequence of the fine open winter, the eggs have hatched in our ponds in 115 days, and have done so corresponding to the days on which the eggs were deposited. Thus the eggs on the 13th of November have hatched on the 8th of March, and have continued doing so in the corresponding days. In former seasons they have taken from 130 to 140 days, according to the temperature of the water. In spring water flowing from the rock in winter, where the temperature is always equal, I have known them to hatch in about sixty days."

Not only does temperature affect the eggs, but also the young fish, for in the second week in February the sun's rays fell at midday almost direct upon my boxes, causing the temperature of the water to rise nearly to 60°. This was too great a heat for the young fish, and the weakest of them began to look very sickly. I however immediately placed a large block of ice in the earthenware tank which supplies their water, and thus lowering the temperature, the fish showed their gratitude by becoming lively again. Luckily I was able to obtain ice quickly, but I thought (while waiting for it) of the experiments in carrying salmon to Australia, and what would have happened if "The Field" window had been the "between-decks" of an Australian clipper just passing through the tropics, and the young fry had just been hatched out of the egg—what grief and sorrow it would have been to their human nurse if he found his stock of ice was all exhausted. Anyhow, we have learnt that the young fry soon begin to pine if the thermometer marks many degrees over 55°.*

The proper temperature of the water both in and out of doors ought to range from 40° to 45°. Mr. Ponder's observations tell him that at this temperature *it requires thirty-five days for the eyes to appear* (*i. e. that the fish is formed in the egg*), *and that they hatch out fourteen days afterwards;* this same result has been obtained by him for two seasons following with very little variation.

Again, he has observed that when the temperature was 50° (in the spring of the year) the eyes of the fish were visible in twenty-six days, and that he hatched then out in ten days afterwards. Lay it down

* See report on experiments carried on by Mr. Youl and myself at the end of the book.

however for an axiom, that the higher the temperature for the egg the weaker the fish produced from that egg,—anything above 50° is weakening.

The first fish again hatched out from a batch are the weakest, the last are the healthiest; when however they once begin to hatch they will come out all in a mass, two, three, or four thousand of a morning. The proper temperature for trout and salmon eggs is 40° to 45°, and again I repeat it, anything over 50° is weakening.

Grayling, however, appear to be an exception to this rule; Mr. Ponder has obtained a fair supply of the ova of these fish, which the Thames Angler Preservation Society are about to introduce into the Thames. The quantity obtained amounted to between fifteen and twenty thousand, and though several of these have died, the remainder promise to do well; they are much more delicate than trout ova, both in appearance and hatching, and seem to die at the least provocation; they are beautifully transparent, and when viewed in the sun of a lovely opalescent hue. He has discovered about these a most interesting and I believe a novel fact. The body of the fish is perfectly visible in *nine days*, and the fish will actually hatch out of the egg in *fourteen days.*

I have some young grayling now at "The Field" office, and most beautiful little things they are. If they get into the boxes with the trout and salmon, these fish will attack and devour them.

YOUNG FISH.

All difficulties and troubles with the eggs having been overcome, we are at length rewarded by seeing the young fish begin to come out of the egg. When I first received the salmon and trout eggs from Hunungue, the eyes of the young fish were just visible as two small jet-black specks—the sign that they will bear transport; the oil globules could also be seen in the substance of the egg, and the tail of the fish could be observed moving from side to side with a rapid vibratory movement. The young fish increased in size daily, and every morning their growth was plainly perceptible; more especially could be noticed the form of the head, and the *darkening* of the transparent substance which would eventually be the body. I have already ascertained one fact, and this (as the question has frequently been put to me) I shall venture now to mention. The eggs do *not* grow—*i. e.*, they do not increase in circumference or in diameter—but the fish *inside* them most certainly increases in bulk, till at last it becomes so large that the egg-shell suddenly bursts, and out comes the young fish.

I have never yet seen a more beautiful sight than the gradual development of the young salmon and trout. We begin with a globule of albumen (or white of egg); we see within it a faint line, and two black spots; day by day these become larger till the young fish is born. Time goes on; the umbilical vesicle is absorbed, the colour appears on the scales, the long single crests which one observes at birth as running down the upper and lower parts of the body, resolve themselves, as it were by magic, into the various fins distinctive of the adult creature, and we have a perfect fish before us. Nature, ever wonderful in her works, surpasses herself in the beauty and minuteness of finish of these little fish.

On the morning of January 14th, White (the viper-catcher, whom I place in charge of my boxes at the "Field"), came up to report to me that the fish were hatching. I immediately went down, and found two of the salmon out of their shells, and quietly reposing among the ova. Sprightly young creatures were these water-babies, not yet two hours old. The moment they saw the spoon with which I wanted to catch them coming near, off they went with a rush and a dart like a full-grown fish, using their tails *only* as a mode of progression. They have, moreover, a heavy weight to carry, for attached to their belly is a large bag, nearly the size of a lemon-pip, but more oblong in shape, which contains the nourishment which they must absorb into their systems before they are able to shift for themselves ; the moment the contents of this forage bag are gone, they at once begin to feed with the mouth, like adult fishes. I removed the new-born fish immediately into the lower trough, which contains gravel. In an instant away they wriggled under a stone, where they reposed in security, their bag helping to keep them down.

A gallant Colonel the other day asked me

a question. "I was walking alongside my river," said he, "when I found a moorhen's nest in the rushes. I took up one of the eggs and broke it, and out came a young moorhen, who looked at me for an instant and then swam away in the greatest haste. Now I want to ask you, Mr. Buckland, how it was that this moorhen chick knew that *I* was not its mother?" In a similar way, I want to know how it is that these tiny water-babies, who are as yet not much more than hardened jelly, should know who is their enemy and who is not. Their whole desire seems to be to obtain concealment, and this because instinct (implanted even in these minute but beautiful little creatures) tells them that if they wish to live they must hide themselves the moment they are born.

Other fish—water insects of forms and shapes to them monstrous and ogre-like—hunt for their young lives; they therefore seek concealment from the dangers that threaten them, and thus help to maintain the existence of their species.

As the fish were hatched they fell through the glass rods upon which they were placed as eggs, and when I paid my daily visit I invariably find the *eggs de*creased in number, but the young ones in the tank below the rods much *in*creased in number. So fast, indeed, did they hatch, that I was obliged to construct a new tank entirely for the young fry. The sickly fish I placed in the tank nearest to the water-pipe, that they might have the first "breath" at the water; I called this the Hospital.

It is most interesting to watch the egg at the moment of hatching. If you have luck, you may happen to be gazing on a particular egg, when of a sudden you will see it split in twain at the part corresponding to the *back* of the fish; you will then see a tiny head with black eyes and a long tail pop out, and you will see the new-born creature give several convulsive shudders in his attempts to quit himself from the now useless egg-shell. (See woodcut.) Poor little fellow! he can't manage to get out—the shell is too tight for him; take, therefore, a soft hair-pencil, press lightly on the egg-shell; he seems to know you are his friend; he gives another vigorous kick or two, and presto! he is free and has commenced life. If we judge from his motions, he *must* enjoy life, for away he swims as fast as his tiny fins and wriggling tail will carry him round and round in a circle, and then plump down he goes to the bottom of the tank and reclines upon his side, breathing freely with his gills for the first time in his life (for when in the egg he does not and cannot breathe). Even at this early period of his existence, he seems to know that a *spoon* is his enemy, for invariably when I place a spoon near him or his brother fish, off they scud; they are aware that one of these days a spoon will be the divider and dissector of their cooked bodies, and think that it is come before its time, and it is high time to be off out of its way.

In my boxes I was enabled to show actually being worked out, under our very eyes, many problems of nature; which problems, when carried out on a large scale in the beds of rivers, are really most important as regards our British salmon fisheries. All my eggs (salmon, trout, salmon-trout, and charr) soon hatched out, and the glass rods upon which they were placed became idle. The whole batch of salmon-trout were gone by February 4, leaving a mass of empty egg-shells in the water ; and the young fish, which have fallen through on to the gravel underneath, were as healthy as possible. They are curious little fellows are these baby salmon-trout. I can see no difference when they are just hatched, between them and the common trout, except in their colour. The mass of young salmon-trout look like a number of drops of the *yellow* barley-sugar ; the common trout, on the contrary, are much more pale in colour and are like drops of *white* barley-sugar. This depends, I find, on the colour of the oil globule in the umbilical vesicle being different. Both kinds of trout are very much more quick and active than the young salmon; when touched with the brush they jump up instantly, like a hare from its form; and having (also like the hare) run in a ring two or three times, drop down again to the bottom. The form of the umbilical bag of the common trout is much more round than that of the salmon, rendering it, therefore, more difficult for the fish to get rid of his egg-case; the little creatures often get their bodies out of the egg, but not their umbilical vesicles, and this seems to annoy them much; and I have every day to lend a hand to lots of these little fellows to enable them to make a decent entrance into their watery world. One of these trout I thus assisted, it struck me, had a very peculiar appearance, something wrong about the head. I put him in a small bottle, and held him to the light. To my astonishment, I found he had pink eyes—yes, regular pink eyes, like a white rabbit; and gentlemen who were with me confirmed my observation. In other respects he was like the other water babies. I was curious to see if he would turn out an albino, for whoever yet heard of an albino *fish?* Unfortunately he soon died.

But of all clumsy performers commend me to the baby charr. Most of the charr eggs persisted in *half* hatching, that is, the young fish protruded his head and great staring eyes out of the egg-shell, and there became a fixture. Every morning I found a lot of these half hatched, gazing stupidly at each other, like a lot of village youths who have tumbled down at the winning-post of that exciting but not elegant race, called "jumping in sacks." The fish are as helpless as the rustics; they cannot get out, they are tied round the neck, and, unless the friendly camel-hair brush is at hand to assist, they die then and there; as though they had just put their heads out, and, not feeling satisfied with their position in life, had resolved to retire before they incurred further trials and temptations. I have hatched altogether, therefore, very few of these young charr; but when they *are* hatched, they are very beautiful little things. The salmon from his birth is a great dandy, and a smart, knowing-looking fish; the trout is also smart and very active, flying about the water like a transparent tadpole; but poor little charr is a delicate one. His body is like a slip of white isinglass; his umbilical vesicle is like a water-drop on a cabbage leaf. He tries his best to live, but he and his brethren more often fail than succeed in the attempt. If, however, they do manage to get through the first few days of their lives pretty well, they are, I think on the whole, afterwards more hardy than the salmon or the trout. There are numbers of them now alive and well in a ditch near Mr. Ponder's hatching boxes at Hampton.

Out of one lot of Rhine salmon which were a first-class lot of eggs, I hatched several, but lost more. The eggs were (if I may use the expression) not strong eggs. The young fish inside attained proper size, and managed to burst his shell; but then he could not uncoil his tail, but gave up his chance, turning white, like a bit of boiled white of egg.

Some of another lot of salmon were strong fish. I woke one of them up, the other day, who was apparently quietly reposing fast asleep on the gravel in the apparatus I had in my barrack room. He jumped up with a start, and went straight at the perforated zinc fence which divided him from the charr eggs; he cleared it (the top is just below the level of the water) like a greyhound. He then charged the next fence, also of zinc (between the charr and the salmon-trout), miscalculated his distance, and ran his head right into one of the holes of the zinc, where it stuck fast till I made him "rein back," touching his nose with the camel-hair brush. The cunning fish then, by swimming round and round, at last found that he could go round the *end of* the zinc (which did not touch the side of the vessel), so he simply "sneaked through the gap" and got well into his place again. The last jump he made was at the end of the upper basin—where the water is made to drop by means of a bit of cotton lamp-wick into the lower basin. Twice did this plucky little salmon go fiercely at (to him) this formidable cataract; twice he fell back again; the third time, however, I helped him over with a lift in the rear with the brush, and he took a tremendous drop in among his cousin salmon, who were hatching out in the basin below; there he now remains, and as he has chosen his own quarters I leave him there, hoping he finds himself better off than before starting on this cross-water steeple-chase.

One of my many visitors to the tanks at "The Field" office was narrating to me how he once caught an enormous salmon in the Tay, weighing some thirty odd pounds; this immediately put the idea into my head to weigh one of *my* salmon. He has, poor little wretch, a deal of way to make up before he arrives at thirty pounds, for at present (four days old) he hardly turns the scale at *two grains.*

By the kindness of Mr. Ashworth, of Cheadle, near Manchester, I am enabled to show you a drawing of the young fish who weigh about two grains, and about two days old. He has also given the following observations as regards the increase of weight in the young salmon :—"The fry, at three days old, is about two grains in weight; at sixteen months old, it has increased to two ounces, or 480 times its first weight; at twenty months old, after the smelt has been a few months in the sea, it has become a grilse of eight and a half pounds, it has increased sixty-eight times in three or four months; at two years and eight months old it becomes a salmon of twelve to fifteen pounds in weight. After which, its increased rate of growth has not been ascertained; but by the time it becomes thirty pounds in weight it has increased 115,200 times the weight it was at first.

"I do not suppose there is any other animal that increases so rapidly, and at so little cost, and that becomes such a valuable article of food."

In various creatures the progress of development is different; thus, for instance, in the *human* baby, the first portion of the body developed is the *lower jaw*, and this for an obvious reason, because the most material want of the baby is to obtain the mother's milk by suction. Now, if the lower jaw were not solid and firm, in vain would it try to suck.

Now, in the case of the fish, nature has kindly packed up all the nourishment that it will want for some six or eight weeks in a neat little bag or parcel, which she has affixed to the body of the fish in such a manner that it shall be gradually absorbed into the general system; the fish does not suck milk like a warm-blooded animal, so its lower jaw is *not* developed. What is then the most important organ to the young fish? He has numerous enemies, and it is his first object to get out of their way. The *eyes*, therefore, are the organs which first arrive at perfection; and they are indeed perfection in this minute, jelly-like creature.

The eye is in perfect working order at the moment of birth, though the rest of the body is far from perfection. The lens of the eye is amply developed, as I proved by placing a dead fish in spirit of wine, and observing that the lens turned white instantly it touches the spirit. Thus I was enabled to see, and accurately to judge of, its size and shape. The lining coats of the eye, moreover, are already at birth painted with that beautiful silver-and-gold lining which the angler will see if he cuts open the eye of the next fish he kills. It is especially well seen in the eye of the cod.

This eye, however well suited for the purposes of avoiding danger, is by no means tolerant of light, a fact which I observed and immediately acted upon, for one day I found to my horror that many of the young salmon (the first lot) in "The Field" apparatus were beginning to die. I immediately lessened their depth of water, and put them in water about an inch and a half, and not four inches deep; but still the little things persisted in dying. I could not at first make out the cause, till at last, having watched them most attentively, I observed that they one and all poked their noses under the stones, as if for concealment; many of them—stupid creatures—even getting their heads so far under these stones that they could not get them out again, and there they remained till next morning, when I found them literally drowned, and with their tails projecting upwards, like the tails of dogs and cats we see drowned in shallow water by that most simple but effective apparatus, a stone and a cord.

I concluded from the actions of these fish that light was unpleasant to them, and that they wanted hiding-places. I recollected, moreover, that one generally sees swarms of such small fish near bridges. I therefore got some bits of zinc and some stones, and built miniature bridges in the tanks. I touched up the salmon one by one, and three out of four of them swam away under the bridges in a moment. The next morning I found but few outlying salmon in the tank, and on lifting up the bridges was pleased to find that my plan had succeeded, and that they found out the bridges, and crept under them for shelter, and there they lay all together like a lot of rats under a barn floor. I remarked, moreover, another result: *before* the fish went under the bridges, they were comparatively pale-looking things, with no colour in their bodies; a few short hours had made all the difference, for three out of four of them had, after they had been out of the light, acquired the regular fish colour, and looked no longer pale and miserable.

I found subsequently that my experiment had succeeded well; for plates of zinc I then substituted bits of common slate, such as are used for roofing houses. These, supported by four stones, form capital "hides" for my young fish, and it is most amusing to see them all run away frightened when I lift up the slate. Broken bits of flower-pots form good hides.

Those who rear young fish should, therefore, above all things, recollect the necessity for making "hides" for the fish.

DEFORMITIES.

Now it is not to be supposed, that out of so many thousand fish we shall not have some cripples; accordingly, among the fish which I have hatched, it is curious to observe these deformities, which, however, I must say, are the exception, and not the rule. Some of these fish have regular humped backs ; others have their bodies twisted round their umbilical vesicle, corkscrew-fashion: and when they see the spoon or the brush coming, or are otherwise alarmed, it is curious to witness their attempts to make a start. They are terrible bad goers, and remind one of the clumsy individuals described by the sailors as "a chap with a kink in his leg." Instead of going forward, they spin round and round, like a "merry-go-round" in a horse-pond. If our crippled friends had been wild fish, they would soon have been snapped up by their kind friends their brother fish, or by some hungry water-beast or other.

My friend Mr. Ponder, thinking, I suppose, that I must be a fish as well as a human doctor, kindly sent me up a bottle full of cripples from his apparatus at Hampton. I have already hatched out a most curious specimen myself, viz., a trout with two heads, and one tail which serves for the two heads, and *one* umbilical vesicle. This double fish is alive and well. Mr. Ponder has sent me not only a similar specimen of a trout (also alive), but also a salmon with one tail and two bodies (a most desirable breed of fish in the eyes of the fishmonger, if we could only manage to cultivate them). He also found among the young fish a charr with four eyes, —a trout with body twisted like a bell-spring, —a trout with a body as round as a ring, besides numerous other deformed patients, fit for the Orthopœdic Hospital, diagrams of some of which I now exhibit, drawn by Mr. W. Searson.

Strange to say, the "monster" fish do not always die. The "Siamese (salmon) twins" are alive and well; they have but one tail between them, and one umbilical bag—and I should imagine but one sentiment common to both, for when one runs, the other runs also, but which of them has the actual command of the tail I am unable to ascertain. It will be curious to see if these fish will ever dissolve partnership. I do not see how they are to do it. If they, however, do make some mutual arrangement, they will, when grown up, be a curious couple indeed; and would, as White (the curator of the tanks) remarks, be "rum 'uns to catch."*

* This double fish is still alive, and I was luckily enabled, by the kindness of Professor Tyndall, to exhibit it (or them) under the electric lamp, when they showed themselves exceedingly vigorous, kicking about famously, to the great amusement of the spectators.

The physiological cause of these double fish, I am at a loss to explain. Both Mr. Ponder and myself, however, are of opinion (until a better reason can be found) that the cause of the *hump-backed* and otherwise deformed fish, is pressure received during their transport in the egg state from Huningue, the soft embryo having been in somewhat bent or damaged by the adjacent moss or eggs. This seems probable, as out of the 27,000 trout eggs which were taken by Mr. Ponder, and carefully carried in water home by hand, and deposited in the boxes a few hours after they were taken, there are *no* cripples and *no* double-bodied fish, but, instead, they are all healthy, straight-backed, active little creatures.

MICROSCOPIC APPEARANCES OF YOUNG FISH.

Let us now see if we cannot learn more about the young fish? Get out the microscope, and place a young, new-born salmon under a low power, and you shall see one of the most beautiful sights ever beheld by human eye. You shall see the tiny heart, which is situate just underneath the lower jaw, going pit-a-pat, pit-a-pat; you shall see the blood at one instant in one cavity of the heart (where it appears like a red speck); at the next instant it is in the other side of the heart; and so it goes on, day and night, never ceasing, never tired—a great forcing-pump, propelling the blood to all parts of the body, and gradually building up the frame of a future king of fishes. I counted the pulse of the salmon when it was under the glass, and ascertained that it averaged about seventy in a minute. My friend, Mr. Hall, of Farningham, has made observations on the pulse of one of his young trout. He reports that, on April 6th, when the fish was just hatched out of the ovum, the pulse was eighty per minute. On the 13th it was ninety-five, and on the 17th, one hundred-and-twelve per minute. Just below the heart can be seen on the umbilical vesicle (when the fish is in the water) a bright red streak; examine this under the microscope, and you will see that this red streak is in fact a main artery; with a high power, you can see plainly the minute blood-discs coursing along between the walls of this elastic tube. The minor red streaks upon the umbilical vesicle can in the same way be made out also to be blood-vessels, containing blood-discs running along at a great pace. Again, down the centre of the transparent body of the fish can be seen, with the unassisted eye, two tiny streaks; the microscope shows that these also are blood-vessels, and that the blood in the one is running towards the head, in the other towards the tail. A more complete and beautiful demonstration of the circulation of the blood never was yet placed under a microscope. The blood in the web foot of a frog is pretty enough; but it is as a school-boy's daub compared to a painting by Sir Edwin Landseer.*

* At this point of the lecture the figures of four or five young fish were exhibited by Professor Tyndall, by means of the electric light. The little creatures were magnified to about two feet long, and kicked about famously ou the whitened

I have already stated that the young fish are nourished by the gradual absorption of the contents of their umbilical vesicle, but there is, I believe, a phenomenon about this which has not hitherto been observed, or, if observed, not carefully examined. I have noticed, and so has Mr. Ponder, that in many of the young fish the umbilical vesicle has two coats or coverings, so that as the contents of the *internal* coat are absorbed, the external coat is seen, (especially at the lower extremity,) hanging loose and empty, so that one sees plainly a bag suspended within a bag.

Again, in the young fish we may clearly perceive the remarkable action of the two

surface on to which the figures were thrown, to the delight of those present, and the great discomfort of the fish themselves.

little pectoral fins; these are moving incessantly day and night, and carefully as I have watched, I have never yet seen them stop for an instant. A curious result followed from this to the little fish which I hatched in my barrack-room; the perpetual motion of the fins collected the bits of dust that were floating in the water, and felted them into a regular collar round the fish's throat. Every morning I caught in a spoon the fish which wore this Elizabethan frill—a touch of the camel-hair brush, and they slipped away out of their collar as merry as ever again.

There are, however, certain points in the economy of the young fish which required interpretation by means of the microscope, viz.: first, the gradual absorption of the contents of the umbilical vesicle into the body of the fish, the one decreasing as the other increases—as well as the curious phenomenon of this vesicle having a double covering; secondly, the perpetual motion of the pectoral fins. I therefore requested my friend, Mr. Henry Hancock, F.Z.S., F.C.S., &c., to undertake a microscopic examination of them, and this gentleman has kindly sent me for publication the following interesting and able paper on the subject, in which several new and important facts are elucidated.

SOME REMARKS RELATIVE TO YOUNG SALMON.

BY HENRY J. B. HANCOCK, F.Z.S., F.C.S.

In January of this present year, it was suggested to the author that he should investigate two points to which, as yet, but little attention has been given, viz.:—1. The motion of the pectoral fin in the fish, whether voluntary or involuntary? 2. The process of nutrition in the young fish, how carried on?

In regard to the first point, viz., the motion of the pectoral fin, it has not, I believe, yet been inquired into, whether this motion, which is incessantly carried on day and night during the life of the fish, be voluntary or not. It has often been conjectured, and with great appearance of truth, to be involuntary; the object of this perpetual motion—viz., to keep a constantly changing stream of water before the mouth and gills of the fish, and to remove that portion which has been deprived of the air contained in it, by the action of the gills of the fish—is intimately connected with the involuntary principle by which all organs engaged in the carrying on of life are actuated.

Having obtained from Mr. Buckland (2nd Life Guards), and from Mr. Bartlett, of the Zoological Society's Menagerie, some young salmon and trout, I proceeded to the investigation by, in the first place, submitting a living fish to the microscope, employing for the purpose a 2-inch object glass. Under this power the muscle could be seen distinctly contracting and expanding as it opened the mouth of the fish and moved the pectoral fin. Having thus ascertained the exact position of the muscle, I proceeded to take a dead fish and dissect it carefully out. Having done so, I submitted it to the microscope, using this time a $\frac{4}{10}$-inch object glass. Under this power the structure of the muscle is plainly visible, and the regular transversely-striated appearance leaves no doubt whatever of its voluntary character. (Object No. 1.)* Not content with this, I proceeded to dissect out one of the pectoral fins of another fish, with a portion of the muscle adhering thereto. In this case also there was no doubt whatever of the voluntary nature of the structure of the muscle. I have also examined the pectoral fin and muscle of the smelt, and find the same striated appearance, and consequently the same voluntary principle.

* These objects, mounted on glass, have been presented to me by Mr. Hancock.

(Object No. 4.) In the sole, also, I remark the same structure. (Object No. 5.)

Although it may be said that the striated structure of the muscle is no *absolute proof* of its voluntary nature, I think that, as there is but one instance of involuntary muscle being transversely striated (I allude to the muscles of the heart), we may fairly conclude that the action of the pectoral fin is purely voluntary. On the other hand, on examining a part of the gill of the young salmon, in which the terminal loopings of the muscle moving it were beautifully shown, I found these muscles (though their fibres were not more than one-third the diameter of those of the pectoral) purely of an involuntary character.

Now, to turn to the second and still more

interesting point in our inquiries, viz., the nutrition of the young fish, how carried on? That is to say, how does the nutriment contained in the umbilical vesicle become absorbed into the body of the fish? This question, interesting as it is, has never before, I believe, been satisfactorily answered. Mr. Buckland showed me a large drawing of a young salmon magnified sixty-six diameters, in which a duct is represented leading out of the umbilical vesicle just above the large oil globule, and tending backwards and upwards into the body of the fish, where it bifurcates and is lost a little above the main artery; asking me to inquire into the matter and find out whether the duct was a fact or not; and if it were truly so, then where it led from and to. To this point I have, then, devoted myself for some time past, and by the invaluable aid of the microscope have, I think, succeeded in unravelling the mystery. After a most careful examination of the living and the dead fish I came to the conclusion that the duct was not there. I found, however, a mark which, cursorily examined, might lead a person to suppose that some duct existed, but across which the circulation was proceeding vigorously ; but of the supposed bifurcated termination of the duct there was no sign whatever. Having discovered what was not, it remained for me to discover what was : I have now to report the result of my investigation.

The umbilical vesicle consists of a double sac containing fatty matter. The inner of the two sacs is covered with a network of veins through which the portal circulation of the fish is carried on; it also contracts as it becomes gradually emptied of its contents. The outer sac, on the contrary, does not contract, and has no circulation over it; in fact, its only purpose seems to be to protect the very delicate inner sac. It appears to be quite insensitive, as the fish is not incommoded by its being cut, whereas he shows discomfort if the inner sac is but touched. The sac contains, besides the fatty matter, three or four loose globules of pure oil. The liver is situated on the right side of the fish, just on the boundary between the body and the umbilical vesicle, rather projecting into the vesicle (as in the human subject the liver of the infant projects beyond the false ribs), as shown in drawing No. 2. On examining the circulation under a high power I was assured of there being matter other than blood corpuscles circulating in the veins, and, on further examination, came to the conclusion that there were globules of fat mixed with the blood. On examining into the course of the circulation I find that the blood is conveyed from the heart (which is visible just under the gills of the fish) into the liver by a branch of the large trunk artery, which, after giving out branches to the intermediate spaces between the ribs, to the kidneys, &c., is finally lost in the ring of muscular fibre in the tail; that from the liver, part proceeds by the large vein, shown in drawing No. 2, straight to the heart; the remainder, after ramifying over the umbilical vesicle of the fish, is finally collected in the large vein (inferior vena cava?) bordering the front part of the vesicle, as shown in No. 1, and returned to the heart, taking with it a portion of the contents of the vesicle received by absorption, which, being transmitted to the liver, is there assimilated and again conveyed to the heart by the large vein, shown in drawing No. 2, for circulation in the body of the fish.

This I consider the right view to take of the mode of nutrition in the young salmon, the idea of the duct being as preposterous as it is incorrect. If, however, I am wrong, I shall still rejoice to have opened a door to discussion on a subject which has hitherto occupied so little consideration amongst men of science.

What eventually becomes of the outer sac of the vesicle I am not in a position to state, not having yet been enabled to examine the fish in a sufficiently forward condition. On a future occasion I hope to be enabled to account for this, as also to state what position the veins of the umbilical vesicle take in the more mature fish.—J. B. HANCOCK.

37, Harley Street, Cavendish Square.

Upon this interesting and important paper the editor of "The Field" remarks :—

The explosion of the fallacy of the mythic duct leading to nowhere, and which formed so striking and peculiar a feature in the previous representations of the embryo on an enlarged scale, is a most valuable fact, as clearing up the difficult points in the circulation of the embryo, the eliciting of which forms a step in our knowledge of these interesting little strangers, for which science should be most grateful to our astute and persevering correspondent, whom we beg to thank for the care and skill he has bestowed on this interesting investigation.

TREATMENT OF YOUNG FISH.

All the young fish having hatched out, my advice is certainly to leave them in the boxes till the umbilical vesicle is absorbed. They do not want any food, as I have before explained, for they are supported by the contents of the umbilical vesicle, and at this time above all others require protection. You may at this time increase your flow of water, as I have discovered, from painful experience, that water which is sufficient for a given number of eggs is not sufficient for the same number of young fish when they come out of the eggs. It is at this time that you will probably lose many young fish from what is called "gill fever." A nasty tenacious white fungus attaches itself to the gills, and in a short time completely obstructs the action. This seems to me to be a regular epidemic among fish, and may be said to be analogous to measles and scarlatina among the young of our own species. You will also observe a fungus growing on the backs of the weakly fish. I know no remedy for these diseases, except separating the fish, that they shall not be overcrowded, causing the stream of water to be increased, and attending to the hides and general cleanliness. By looking to these points you will save many fish, both in your outdoor and indoor boxes.

The time will soon arrive when the fish will require feeding. When the umbilical bag is empty they will begin to feed by the mouth, and at this time if you do not feed them, they will peck at each other's tails, (or, as White says, " will fly at each other like a parcel of little bull-dogs,") and be long, lanky in the body, with great bull-dog like heads. The French authorities recommend at this time that they should be fed with the boiled flesh of frogs powdered into minute bits. The Stormontfield authorities use boiled liver, powdering it in their hands, and throwing it in. You must, however, take care that it does not accumulate at the bottom of the water, and thus imbue it with putrescent matter. I should recommend that the fish always be fed at a given spot, and that a bit of cloth, or even a tin tray, or other material should be placed at the bottom of the water, at the spot where they are fed, so that you can occasionally lift it out, and with it all the bits of food not devoured by the fish. There is another way of feeding the fish which is very neat and commodious. Get from the fishmongers the fresh roe of the sole, plaice, whiting, or other small sea-fish, it must not be salted, and must not be the least decayed. Mix it up with a stick in clean water, and put a little of the water among the fish. You will see that the un-divided eggs comprising this roe separate themselves, and are just the right size for the fishes' mouths. They will, if hungry, snap them up greedily. But do not put in too great a quantity at a time. The fish too, be it remarked, feed best at early morning.

Again, you may try if they will eat minute water insects, red worms, &c.; they certainly like minute flies, for "Peter of the Pools" writes as follows :—

"After the bag was absorbed they became very handsome little fish, but we were quite puzzled how to feed them, as we could not devise any food small enough for them to swallow. We tried them with trout roe and several other substances, but we found all too large for them, and they must have lived on some small animalculæ which kept them alive; but, although the little fish were brisk, they grew very slowly indeed after the bag was absorbed. They were supplied every day with fresh water from the Tay, running through a tap. They were hatched in the beginning of April, and in June some of them were getting larger. I had then the skin of an enormous eel, about seven or eight feet long, which had been sent me (with a grilse that it had swallowed) from Mr. Buist's fishings in the Isle of Skye. This was in the year 1831. When the weather got very warm, the skin of the eel, from which an oily substance oozed out, was found covered every morning with small midges, as thick as fur on a lady's boa. This was shaken over the tub, when the little fish sprang up and swallowed them greedily. Numbers of the fish were found dead, with small black swellings like balls in their stomachs, which when they were opened, and the balls spread out under a microscope, were found to be the dead flies packed closely together. The fish were therefore more sparingly fed with them, and, so far as food went, seemed to be healthy."

Acting on this hint, I obtained through the kindness of Mr. Hall of Farningham, a bottle full of minute gnats which he caught in his hall window, and placing them by means of a moistened brush on the top of the tanks in "The Field" office window, was pleased to see the young salmon and trout rise freely at them as they floated down the stream, making a twist and boil of the water exactly like their fathers and mothers in their native mountain torrents: this is a most interesting and amusing sight, inasmuch as the spectator sees in miniature exactly what happens on a grand scale when he is angling for the full-grown fish in their native wild and rapid streams. The young fish is seen in mid-water, gently holding his own by movements of the tail; the fly comes over him, his tail begins to "wag," and in an instant he darts like an arrow from a bow, upwards in an oblique direction, and takes the fly so instantaneously that the eye cannot observe the action; then comes that peculiar twist and twirl in the water so well known to all fishermen, and which is made by the tail giving force to the *descent* of the fish back again into the deep. Again, in the tanks before us we see going on exactly what Mr. Francis has described in "The Field" as happening on a large scale in the Thames.* The trout and

* "I can always tell where fish are to be found, if there are any, because there are certain places—big stones, precipitous banks, &c.—which are favourable resting places; and where such places are, there is certain to be a fish. Catch one, and in due time another will certainly fill his place; and the most singular part of the thing is, that they will always be fish of near about the same size. The pile I allude to is such a place, and the fish that hang about it are always about five or six pounds weight; it is known as 'the white pile,'—a pile at the end of the small eyot at Sunbury; lower down, towards the cherry orchard, there is always a fish of some eight pounds; at the orchard there is always a heavy fish; off the water-works there is always a fish of seven or eight pounds. At Hampton Court weir, when I fished it formerly, there was a corner where, if

salmon each chooses his own quarters—behind a stone, just at the edge of the slate, under a certain bit of weed, &c., and on his domain he allows no other fish to trespass, on any pretence whatever. There is one salmon in particular, who has chosen the spot where the water falls into the tank, and he is *always* there, close under the fall. White reports of him that he does not allow any other

ever you caught or saw a fish, he was always a whopper—the biggest in the weir. I have known more than a dozen fish taken from that corner during several years, and not one of them weighed less than nine or ten pounds. This is a very extraordinary fact, nevertheless it is a fact; and those old observant fishermen on the Thames who really know 'what is what,' will bear out what I say in this respect, I am sure. The same thing occurs with salmon. There are certain casts for big fellows which no little one presumes to trespass upon, and certain casts for smaller potentates. In smaller trout-streams the same law holds good to the very letter, as every fly-fisher of any experience will verify. Now, it is to increase the number of these 'likely places' by dropping in big stones, lumps of old brick-work, &c., that I am advocating.

"FRANCIS FRANCIS."

fish near him, and flies at and bites them when he sees them coming; he does not even spare the young grayling that escape from the tank above. These he will "carry about in his mouth like a cat does a mouse."

The young salmon and trout certainly eat the young grayling when they can catch them, for they are very active; they also eat young perch. I have placed perch spawn in their tanks, and as the perch, which are exceedingly minute, hatch out, they are caught up and devoured in an instant.

TURNING OUT FISH.

A great question now arises as to turning out the fish into the streams, *i.e.*, at what period they should be let loose into the waters, which the rearer of them wishes to stock. Upon this point authorities differ. Mr. Ashworth, in a letter to myself, expresses himself as being of the opinion that if they are turned out at once (*i.e.*, when they begin to feed), they will, from various causes, be lost to the river. Both he and the Stormontfield authorities always keep their young fry in ponds, and feed them till they put "on their jackets;" *i.e.*, assume the smolt coat, and go of their own accord to the sea. It must be recollected that the conditions of the waters of the regular salmon rivers are very different to those of the Thames. But, however, depend upon it Messrs. Ashworth and Buist are right in their opinions, practical men as they are, as regards the salmon.

Mr. Ponder and Mr. Francis Francis are, I know, in favour of turning the fish out *into the Thames* at once—*i.e.*, when they begin to feed—and this because, if the fish is turned down in a state of babyhood, he has to "graduate through all his difficulties," and learns to shift for himself; whereas, if kept as a semi-tame fish for several months, when turned down he goes gaping out till Master Jack comes and gobbles him up, and "is dead" (as the Yankees say) "before he knew what had hurt him." Anyhow, I have a curious fact to mention. When Mr. Ponder was repairing the boxes towards the end of last year, getting ready for this year's ova, he found three or four young fish (hatched out last season) which had been residing *under* the boxes since they were hatched. These fish are now a good four inches long, and good healthy-looking fellows. We know not for certain how the fish in the Thames are getting on, but the river-keeper (Melborne) has told Mr. Ponder that he has seen several young trout in the shallows. If this be the fact, rejoice, ye Thames anglers, and encourage pisciculture!

Some few weeks ago Mr. Ponder invited me to assist him in turning out a large batch of young salmon and trout. We let them loose into quiet, lone, undisturbed shallows,* too shallow for perch and jack (which, by the way, were spawning, and therefore

* The fish are all turned into those parts of the Thames which are under the management of "The Thames Angling Preservation Society," and which, therefore, are never netted. See the laws of the Society; and if you are an angler, help their praiseworthy efforts to afford good angling sport to all.

weakly when we turned in our young fish) Each fish immediately sought out a resting or a hiding place, behind a stone or bit of weed—for be it remarked as a curious fact, that young trout are *not gregarious*—and there he took up his position as happy as a fish could be. As regards what became afterwards of these very fish, Mr. Ponder writes me thus:—"Among the advantages of early turning into the river must be reckoned that of rapid growth. Some of those which you and I turned in were, after only *nine days*, found to be *three or four times larger* than those of same age left behind in the troughs."

Andrew, the keeper, has also seen several of these young trout on the shallows at a different place. "One of these," he says, "would weigh down four of the fish now in the boxes." We have, however, a ditch at Hampton, about two feet deep, which conducts the water from the hatching boxes into the river. About ten yards of this is shut in by perforated zinc, and several of the fish have dropt down into the nursery from the boxes above. They seem to be doing very well, and are useful for observation's sake; but of course they require feeding, in addition to what minute food they get in the ditch.

My advice, therefore, to experimenters, as regards the Thames and other southern waters, is to turn out with a gentle hand the young fish on to quiet and undisturbed shallows in the main river; or else into an *ever-flowing* (not stagnant), broad, weed-containing pond or ditch, whence the young fry can escape into the stream when they please. It is also advisable to keep some of them in a ditch, containing from one to three feet deep of flowing (not rapid) water, for the sake of comparing them with the fish that have been turned out into the open. A water-cress bed is a capital place. Recollect always they are not to be turned down till the umbilical bag is absorbed, and they require food.

As regards the turning out question, when it refers to salmon, and salmon only, I have no positive experience myself, and must therefore beg to refer my readers to an admirable little book on salmon breeding by Wr. William Brown, of Perth; also the Messrs. Ashworth's treatise,* which is full of the re-

* A Treatise on the Propagation of Salmon and other Fish. By Edward and Thomas Ashworth. London. Simpkin and Marshall. 1853. Price (I think) 1s.

sults of practical experience, and which gives illustrations of many matters which will be useful to the experimenter.* The columns of "The Field" also abound with correspondence on this matter, and they are always open to information and discussion on this and other matters relating to fish breeding and angling.

Whether the young fish be retained in the boxes, turned into a ditch, or kept in ponds, it will always be remarked that some individuals grow more rapidly and attain a greater size than others. As a remarkable example of this fact, I give an instance.†

* Natural History of the Salmon, as ascertained by the recent experiments on the artificial spawning and hatching of the ova, and rearing of the fry, at Stormontfield, on the Tay. Thos. Murray and Son, Glasgow; Paton and Ritchie, Edinburgh; Arthur Hall, Virtue, and Co., London. Price 2*s.* 6*d.*

† See "The Field," April 25, 1863.

"Sir,—As another instance in the strange anomaly in the growth of salmon, I send you three specimens taken from the Stormontfield pond on April 1. As the label on the bottle tells, they were spawned from salmon roe about the end of December, 1861; they came to life and were hatched in April, 1862; they have been fed in the same pond, and you will observe what an amazing difference there is in the size and growth, the largest being $6\frac{1}{2}$ inches, and weighing 646 grains; the second $3\frac{5}{8}$ inches, weighing 135 grains; and the third $2\frac{1}{8}$ inches, weighing 26 grains.

"You will observe that No. 3 is a tiny little creature with the parr marks on it; No. 2 has the incipient scales on it; and No. 1 with these scales far advanced. I have no doubt that at least No. 1, had he been left in the

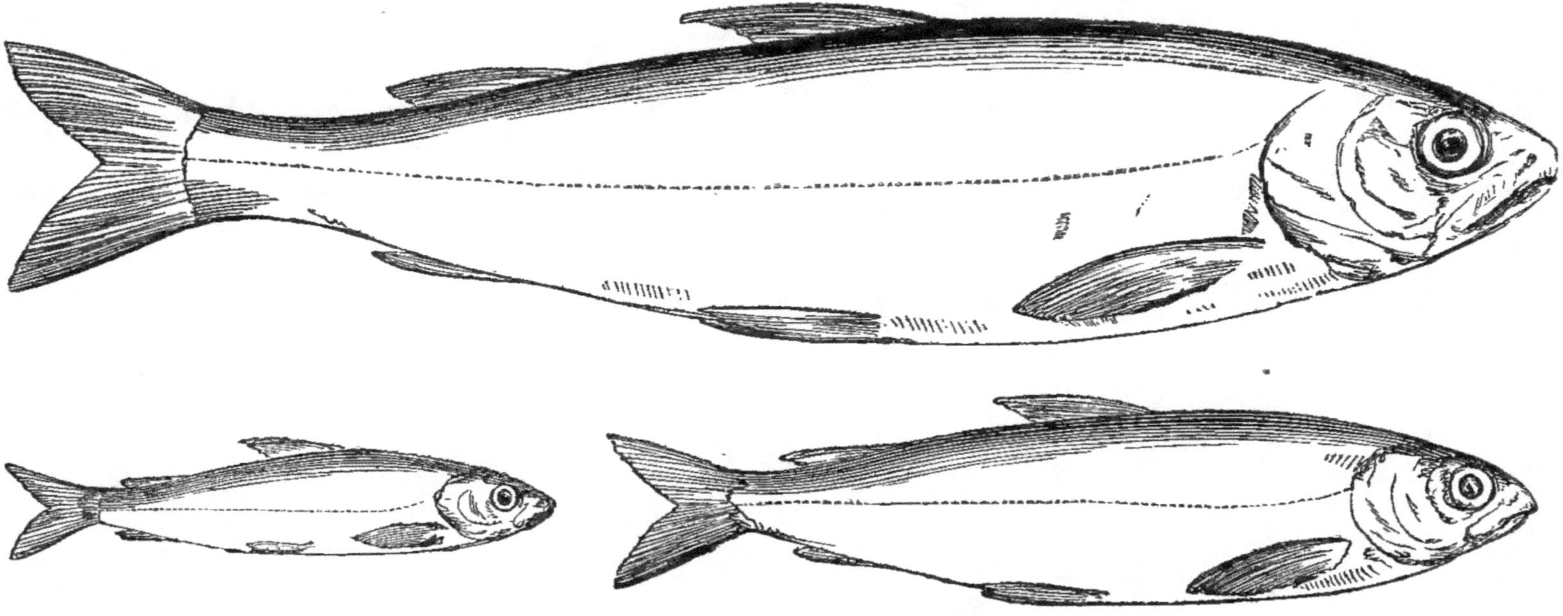

THREE PARRS OF THE SAME AGE FROM STORMONTFIELD.

ponds, would, with others of like size, or even smaller, have gone to the sea this year, and returned as a grilse. No. 2 is doubtful, and may perhaps have remained till another season; while No. 3, would we allow him, would keep his habitation in the pond. However, as I formerly mentioned, as we have only one feeding-pond, we must turn them all out as we had such a small crop last year, to make room for their younger brethren, far more numerous, that are getting into existence. I trust by this time next year we shall have a second pond, by which we will be able to breed every year; as at present, owing to about one half going off the first year, we cannot leave the other half in the pond, as they would destroy the brood of the second spawning season.

"You will be so good as to show these to Mr. Buckland, as I would be glad to have such an eminent naturalist's opinion on this strange anomaly.

"PETER OF THE POOLS."

To this—thanking "Peter of the Pools" for the compliment—I replied as follows:—

"I am exceedingly obliged to 'Peter of the Pools' for allowing me the opportunity of examining these most interesting fish, of which, by the kindness of the Editor, outline figures are given, in order that the very marked difference in size between them can be seen by those who have not the opportunity of examining the specimens themselves. The drawings are given of an accurately-measured life-size. Now for the cause of the phenomenon. On Tuesday evening last, I submitted the specimens and letter from 'Peter of the Pools' to the scientific meeting of the Zoological Society. J. Gould, Esq., F.R.S., and Dr. Günther, of the British Museum, were much pleased with the facts narrated, and, after a considerable discussion, gave it as their opinion that, provided always the evidence of their being of the same age is well proved, this was simply a case of cause and effect—the bigger fish being the stronger and most healthy of the lot. I myself quite agree with this: a number of fish are turned out simultaneously into a pond; some are weak, some are strong; the stronger, of course, gain the mastery over their brethren, and gain all the advantages of the pond, whatever those advantages may happen to be; the consequence is, that, in proportion to their advantages they become larger than those which have them not. The same thing happens in, so to say, human ponds; for in large cities we find that the babies and young children who are well fed and live in good air are much stronger and healthier—ah, and for the most part larger too, than those born and bred in crowded courts and back passages, and who feed on red herrings and tea rather than on butchers' meat and beer. Take a given number of children from a given large city, say a hundred of the same age, and put them side by side. I doubt not that we should be able to pick out three specimens from among them whose full-length photographs, if grouped together, shall show as much difference as do the drawings of the three fish now before the reader. A naturally stronger constitution, a better supply of food, and other minor advantages, will make all the difference both in the size of human beings and also in the size of fish; and this law will apply to nearly all races of animals. If, again, we find, what is not uncommon among ourselves, viz., a specimen of 'a little old man,' why should not we also find 'a little old fish?'

"After the meeting of the Zoological Society, I next morning carefully dissected the fish in the bright sunlight and under clear pure water, for I like always to look into the insides as well as the outsides of specimens; not only for information's sake, but because it adds additional value to their history.

"I was rewarded for my pains, for I discovered a great difference in the contents of the stomach of these three fish. No. 1 contained a great quantity of small water-shells, and nothing else whatever. No. 2 contained not a single shell, but a quantity of insects, principally winged black ants, midges, and those peculiar black flies who seemed to delight in committing suicide in the eyes of human beings. The stomach of No. 3 contained nothing, or positively next to nothing; anyhow I could not make out what it was. A lawyer arguing the case might take this difference in food as evidence of the cause of the difference of the growth of these fish. Anyhow, dissection proves the fact, that the food is different as regards fish Nos. 1 and 2; and this, combined with the arguments above stated, will, I think, enable us to agree that the cause of the phenomenon sent by 'Peter of the Pools' is simply difference of natural vigour, and also of food, in these three different-sized young salmon.

"I have taken the specimens, which I have put up again in the bottle, to 'The Field' office, that those interested in the subject may examine for themselves both the external as well as the internal appearances.

"FRANK BUCKLAND."

TRANSPORT OF OVA AND FISH.

Now, we must not be selfish in our fish-hatching experiments, particularly if we obtain a good hatch of fish. We must think of our friends and neighbours who have waters, and require fish to stock them. The question now arises, How are we to send them fish, so that they shall get to their destination alive and in good health ?

First, recollect eggs are easier to transport than the young fish, and if properly managed may be sent very long distances.

The question of the transport of eggs has been a grave matter with the authorities at Huningue, whose business is to distribute eggs. I have myself (as also have many other gentlemen) received liberal consignments of eggs of various fish from Huningue, and they have arrived in perfect safety.

The newly-taken eggs are placed in their hatching-boxes at Huningue, and there allowed to develop themselves till the *eyes of the fish are plainly seen in the egg* (see Frontispiece). Then, and not till then, can you move the eggs. If you attempt to do so *before* the eye is seen they will most assuredly die. Wait, therefore, till you see the eyes developed in the eggs you wish to send away.

The following is the best mode of proceeding:—Procure some wide-mouthed bottles, three or four inches high—common pickle-bottles or tumblers will do very well;—place at the bottom of the bottle or tumbler a layer of fresh moss (this must have been well washed previously), then dip it in clean cold water, and squeeze the superfluous water out, so that the moss shall be wet, but not dripping. Portions of rough sponge, the size of a wallnut, well cleaned, are as good packing as moss, and are cleaner (these must also, of course, be damped). Upon the layer of moss deposit a layer of your "eye-showing" eggs, and arrange them so that they shall not touch one another. Place another layer of moss, another layer of eggs, and so on till the bottle is full; but there must be no pressure anywhere. Pour out any water that has collected at the bottom of the bottle, cover the top with a bit of common paper, and stab some holes in it with a penknife. Your bottles being all filled, get a stout but light box—arrange your bottles in it in the most convenient position, and stuff them down quite tight with moss that is dripping wet with water, put the cover on the box and fasten it securely. Then place this box inside another box, leaving about two or three inches of interspace. Fill this up quite tight with wet moss, and send them off by the quickest route of transport to your friend. If possible, give them in charge to a friend, or the guard of the train, and avoid exposing them to heat or to cold. This is the mode used at Huningue with so much success. The boxes from Huningue to London usually occupy from two to four days in their travels, if the railway officials attend to the urgent directions on the box, which they do not always do. A letter appeared in "The Times" by Mr. Francis on this point. I have re-packed a box, or rather boxes, which those who call at "The Field" office can see and examine.

Tell your friend directly he receives the eggs to pick the moss out carefully with a pair of forceps, and to place the eggs immediately into the apparatus, which should be all ready to receive them. If it be possible, I advise that the eggs, still packed in the bottles, should be "placed upright" in the boxes for a couple of hours, the water *not* by any means allowed to get into them. The eggs will thus gradually assume the temperature of the water in which it is hoped they will hatch out. A *sudden* change from the hot box to the cold water is not good for the eggs. All the moss must be cleaned off the eggs when placed in the boxes; they may indeed be first turned into a basin, and then gently removed with a common spoon into the boxes, and placed either on the glass rods or on the gravel.

Of course, you will often have to go long distances to obtain the eggs in the first instance from the parent fish. When you have got them at the river side, treat them with the most tender hand, and never let them be exposed for an instant to the air; carry them home in pure cold water, either in large uncut decanters or in a common fish-kettle. *Carry them in your hand*, to avoid shaking, and change the water by dipping it out with a cup (so that the eggs shall not dance about) about every three or four hours. If they have to remain all night at a place, open the cover of the fish kettle, and place them in a tub of cold, fresh spring or pump water which does not contain iron or other injurious chemical solution.

The young fish can also be carried long distances, and this in almost any kind of vessel. It is not necessary to keep these vessels steady; moderate splashing of the water helps to oxygenate it. Change the water as often as you can, say every two or three hours; and if you see the fish getting sickly, blow air into the water by means of a common pair of kitchen bellows, or by means of an ordinary shilling pewter squirt; or use the admirable, simple, and inexpensive aërating apparatus sold by Mr. Wright, fishing-tackle maker, of 376, Strand, which the transporters of live-bait for jack-fishing have found so useful.

I have sent away from my boxes at "The Field" office several parcels of young fish (both before and after the umbilical bag has disappeared from them) to gentlemen who have fisheries. Thus, a noble Duke took with him to Scotland about a hundred grayling and some charr (from Mr. Ponder's). Many of the grayling died from simple and unavoidable causes, and my own neglect in not giving *written* instructions to servants. The charr arrived in safety. My friend Viscount Powerscourt took with him some great lake trout, to stock a newly-formed pond at his estate at Powerscourt, Enniskerry, Ireland.

My friend Captain Berkeley, 2nd Life Guards, also took several great lake trout, salmon, charr, &c., into Oxfordshire; besides, Messrs. Hall, of Farningham; King, of Watford; and several others. The mode of transport adopted was common pickle bottles, or small bait cans, three parts full of water, carried by the person who wishes to transport them. The water was frequently half poured out and fresh added, and air blown into it, on the journey. Young fish thus transported do very well, if properly cared for. On arrival, place them, bottles and all, into the running stream, that the change of temperature be not too great. Of course, with the ordinary chances of war, some of the young fish will die.

To show what a great distance young fish will travel, I must mention that I received a few weeks since some young salmon all the way from Gothenburg, in Sweden. Through the kindness of a correspondent of "The Field," "Gothenburger," we read thus:—

LIVE SALMON FROM GOTHENBURG, SWEDEN.

SIR,—Two days ago I visited my salmon-breeding ponds, and found the ova in an advanced condition. I brought home a few dozens and placed them in a jar, with the intention of forwarding them to you duly packed in moss. This morning I have found the greatest part already hatched, and, thinking it might prove of interest to you to see how the experiment turns out, I send you the fry and the ova, to the number of twenty-seven, inclosed in a jar containing water and river weeds. The jar leaves per steamer for Hull this evening, and will be forwarded by rail, so as to reach you on Monday evening or Tuesday morning. The captain has orders to put a small lump of ice into the jar by mid-day, and to change the water every morning.

The success of my breeding operations this season has been very extraordinary; two days ago I took out 300 ova with a ladle, among which I could only pick out two addled, showing a return of 99⅔ per cent. I will add that the salmon in my river are acknowledged to be the best in Sweden for strength, colour, and flavour.

GOTHENBURGER.

Gothenburg, April 10.

[The readers of "The Field" will, I am sure, join me in thanking "Gothenburger" for his kindness in sending us living specimens of his Swedish salmon. They arrived perfectly sound and well late on Monday evening, the 13th. There were twenty-six live fish, and one egg on the point of hatching out. I have caused a careful drawing of this to be made by an experienced artist, as the characteristics of the salmon egg, with the young fish inside, are so distinctly seen in its clear and beautiful amber-coloured structure. The vessel they came in is simply a gigantic water-bottle; and much credit is due to the captain of the Hull steamer and the railway officials who took such care of it during its voyage from Gothenburgh. They are healthy little fellows, somewhat larger and finer than the Scotch or Irish salmon.—FRANK BUCKLAND.]*

* I regret to say these salmon, though very healthy at first, died away one by one. The heat of the mid-day sun upon the boxes was fatal to them; but they would have lived if I had had better and cooler water to place them in.

As the reader probably is aware, great efforts have been made to transport salmon to Australia, and the Australian Government has voted large sums of money for this purpose. I believe the key to success has been discovered at last: it is "freezing the ova." By the kindness of Mr. Youl, who has the management of the experiments, I have been able to assist in these experiments, which are so important and promise so great results, that I have given them in detail and in consecutive form in the Appendix, for the benefit of future observers. This is *the* question of the day in the transport of useful fish for long distances.

WHAT HAS BEEN DONE, AND WHAT REMAINS TO BE DONE.

Thus far, then, I have endeavoured to show how the eggs may be taken under human care—how they may be protected from their various enemies—how they may be hatched out, and how the young fish should be reared.

It remains now for me to show some results of all this, that it may not be imagined that this is a mere toy, a mere scientific plaything, but a Science as yet in its infancy, and from which the greatest results may be expected.

We must, of course, give preference to the magnificent establishment at Huningue, near Basle, a noble example of what has been already done, by perseverance and energy in a good cause. I have never been to Huningue myself, but when my friend Mr. Coumes, Engineer-in-chief of the works on the Rhine, and also of those at Huningue, came to England, he kindly gave me a series of large and beautifully-executed photographs of the buildings and of the apparatus used, so that the observant spectators can see the whole process as it were before them. It is in this wonderful establishment that the eggs of fish are kept, and advanced in their hatching till they arrive at the period at which they will bear travel. It is by these means that many rivers in France are actually re-peopled with fish, employment given to hundreds of poor fishermen, and the food of the people greatly increased. In order that the reader may see what a vast amount of good has been done by the French authorities, and what a great example they show to England, I would mention that the fish cultivated are as follows :—

1. Truite commune.
2. Truite saumonee.
3. Truite grande des lacs.
4. Saumon du Rhin.
5. Ombre chevalier (Charr).
6. Ombre commune (Grayling).
7. Saumon du Danube.
8. Fera.

The number of these eggs distributed is something enormous. In the year 1861, the total quantity of eggs of these fish distributed was no less than *sixteen million, four hundred and forty thousand, four hundred.**

* I trust to have the returns of 1863 before I go to press with this little book.

Working hard and enthusiastically in the cause of the improvement of fisheries are several French scientific gentlemen, to whom the highest possible praise should be accorded by the English people. Need I mention the name of M. Coste, who having arranged a system for the artificial propagation of both marine and fresh-water fish (see his reports and publications) is, as it were, the father of pisciculture; and of that liberal-minded man, Mr. Coumes, the engineer of Huningue, who has so liberally distributed so many thousand eggs of fish throughout Her Majesty's dominions during the last season, and to whom we owe the greatest acknowledgments, as well as to the French Government, which makes distributions of the eggs of the best kinds of fish gratuitously to all the proprietors of rivers in France who will undertake to hatch and protect them, and make a return of the quantity so produced. I should here record my vote of thanks, and I am sure other recipients will second it, for the large number of sixty-five thousand eggs which have been distributed, since September last, to myself and to owners of various private fish-hatching boxes here in England. I give in the Appendix, by Mr. Ashworth's kindness, Mr. Coumes' report, which will be read with interest, and show upon what an enormous scale the French Government are carrying out the science of fish-hatching.

I must now mention what has been done in England by my excellent friend, Thomas Ashworth, of Cheadle, Cheshire, who in conjunction with his brother, are the owners of the Galway fishery, and who have literally re-peopled with salmon various streams that previously had no salmon in them, as well as a district of their fishery of thirty miles long by ten wide. They have also opened up a great extent of water, viz., a great number of tributary streams from the Claregalway river, up as high as Ballyhaunis. The reader should look at a map to be able to appreciate what a great district is thus rendered productive of salmon.

It will be remembered that the Messrs. Ashworth commenced artificial propagation of salmon at Oughterard, in Galway, the same season that the French commenced at Huningue, neither party being aware of what the other was doing at the time. I quote Mr. Ashworth's own words.

The district of Loughs Mask and Corrib comprise an area of thirty miles long by ten wide, containing 25,000 acres of water, and receive the waters of some of the finest tributaries known for the purpose of propagation. These loughs and tributaries lie to the north of the Corrib, between Joyce's country, in Connemara, and Ballyhaunis, County Mayo; and what is very singular, that while these lakes discharge their contents into Lough Corrib, and the Corrib has an abundance of prime salmon; strange to say, not a single one has ever been found in these upper lakes. Owing to a natural barrier of rocks extending between the two lakes, an obstruction has been put to the progress of the fish, and although a pass has been recently constructed there to facilitate their ascent, and the gates of the pass left open from October to April, it was all to no purpose—not a single salmon was known to have passed up. But that there may be no failure, so far as human means can go, in filling the Mask with fish, men have been employed in stocking its several tributaries with spawn by artificial propagation; and as the fact is now established that the salmon species, after visiting the sea, return to the same rivers in which they had been bred, there can be no doubt that, in a short time, as these experiments have proved successful, this extensive district will be thoroughly stocked with this valuable fish. All that will be required will be proper protection, and in a short time Loughs Mask and Carra, like Lough Corrib, will afford ample sport and pleasure to tourists, and become a fertile source of profit to the community.

At least 659,000 salmon ova were collected, impregnated, and transported into these rivers in December, 1861, from the adjoining streams of Claregalway, where the parent fish are found in great abundance. The process of collecting the ova or egg of the parent fish, as heretofore, has been entrusted to that eminent pisciculturist Mr. Ramsbottom. The operation is very simple, and perfectly harmless to the parent fish.

In order to show how easily the operation of propagation may be performed, Mr. Ramsbottom procured at Abbey, in four hours, over 170,000 ova. The 659,000 salmon eggs which he procured were transported and deposited in gravel beds selected for the purpose, in the purest small streams of the rivers at Tourmakeady, Robe River, at Hollymount, and other rivers connected with Loughs Mask and Carra, were safely hatched out, and are now migrating to the sea (in April, 1863,) in thousands. If the proprietors of similar waste and unproductive rivers would adopt this process, there can be no doubt they would vastly increase the productiveness of their salmon rivers and fisheries. What is wanted, is to stock the breeding grounds well; and to do this effectively, it is indispensable to protect the parent fish during the breeding season.

We cannot be surprised that this important branch of science should have been taken up with avidity, and prosecuted with energy, by so many nations and peoples, when we consider the pecuniary advantages that flow from the system, in a commercial point of view. If to the first cost of an animal reared and fattened on a farm, we add the risks that are run in maintaining him in health and condition until he is fit for human food, the profit for feeding is not very great; but in the case of the salmon, we can send a fish down to the sea, which, even by this artificial means, does not cost a farthing, and he there grows and fattens, without either care or superintendence, without cost or trouble of any kind, and when he is in the highest condition, he returns to us worth about as much as a prime fed sheep, which has required to be watched and cared for till it reached that condition. Here, then, as Lord Essex said, "is a mine of wealth under water, as much as any under ground," and if this be not a branch of public wealth that deserves cultivating, we know of none that is.

Mr. Ashworth, confident as he is himself, told me that he could breed salmon easier and at a much less cost than he could lambs. He has continued his exertions, and in December last Mr. Miller, the Messrs. Ashworth's resident superintendent, collected and deposited no less than *seven hundred and seventy thousand salmon ova* in the streams of Lough Mask, with those of last year, making a total of *one million four hundred and twenty-nine thousand ova.* But in addition to this large supply, Mr. Miller has conveyed *forty adult salmon alive,* a distance of twenty-three miles in a large tub of water, and by frequently renewing the water on the way, they arrived as lively at the end of their journey as they were at the beginning. Those were the first salmon that had ever been known to inhabit the River Robe, a tributary of Lough Mask. More than this; in order to enable these young fish to migrate to the sea, *it was necessary that a fish passage extending about two miles in length* should be made over the rocky ground between Loughs Corrib and Mask. This great undertaking has since been successfully completed by the Messrs. Ashworth, at a cost of upwards of 650*l.*, under the able direction of Mr. Roberts, C.E., by which means salmon are now enabled to pass up and down freely, and they have already been seen in the fish passage or stairs, and have deposited their ova on fords within the new passage, and thousands of smolts are migrating from Mask to the sea, April, 1863.

These are great results. The reader may like to know what is the cost of the artificial hatching of these fish. Mr. Ashworth tells me, the total cost of placing the *seven hundred and seventy thousand* salmon eggs in the fish nests or hatching boxes, and of transporting the salmon, has been *eighteen pounds,* in addition to the regular and weekly cost of his staff of water-bailiffs and workmen.

In order that the reader may appreciate what the actual bulk of these 770,000 salmon ova would be, if all collected together, I would beg to mention that my ingenious-minded friend, J. Lowe, Esq., has calculated the number of individuals which composed the dense crowd that assembled to welcome the Princess of Wales on her arrival in London: figures calculated out on given data give us the number of human beings then assembled at 700,000. Imagine a salmon for each human being, and you will have an idea of the number of fish Mr. Ashworth has hatched out as a stock for his fisheries.

The fisheries have benefited by his exertions to an enormous extent. There are twenty fish now to be seen, where there was one before. The little fish go down to the sea, and come back big fish—good, marketable food, and the balance at the banker's is increased in proportion.

Scotland also has done much for her

fisheries. The establishment at Stormontfield, on the Tay, is now a household word, and the observations, both practical and scientific, made by Messrs. Buist and Brown, are of the greatest importance. I must again refer to the little book by Mr. Brown above mentioned, merely stating that the number of ova placed down this year has been no less than two hundred and seventy-five thousand, and that not including the original cost of the boxes, &c. The working expenses have been under fifty pounds.

I give in the Appendix the latest report of the proceedings at Perth.

As regards the money value to the proprietors of the Tay from the products of this fish-hatching establishment, I quote from Mr. Brown's book.

"The question that now remains to be considered is, 'Has the artificial propagation, even on the small scale that has been carried on at Stormontfield, been of advantage to the fishery proprietors on the Tay. We have no doubt on the matter, for, on referring to a statement of the rental of the Tay published by the proprietors themselves, we find that in the year 1828, the year of the passing of Home Drummond's Act, the rental was *fourteen thousand five hundred and seventy-four pounds.* It gradually fell off every year afterwards till 1852, when it reached the minimum, amounting to *seven thousand nine hundred and seventy-three pounds, five shillings.* In 1853 the artificial rearing commenced; and in 1858, when the statement was printed, the rental was *eleven thousand four hundred and eighty seven pounds, two shillings and five pence:* it has now, 1862, reached what it was in 1828. We are aware that other reasons are given for the rise in the rental, such as the extra price of the fish in the London market, but we should like to know how it happens that all the other rivers in Scotland (with the exception, perhaps, of the Sutherland rivers) which have the same market for their fish, have, since 1852, had a lower rental, instead of an increased one.

"To take the money value of salmon fisheries in the aggregate, and to show what an important question is before us, I now give the following facts, which I have on the best authority :—

ENGLAND

Produces annually about *ten thousand pounds* in money value.

SCOTLAND

Is supposed to produce fish worth in money value nearly *half a million of pounds.*

IRELAND.

The aggregate money value of the salmon fisheries of Ireland at present, by the Report of the Commissioners, is stated to be *three hundred thousands pounds* annually." *

These are astounding figures. We Englishmen in this matter are indeed a long way behind-hand. Mr. Ashworth gives the following important facts in a letter to myself. The extent of rivers in England is much greater than in Ireland: it is supposed that

* See "Report of Commissioners of Fisheries."

they do not produce more than about *ten thousand pounds* per annum, if so much. There is a district in Yorkshire above 600 miles of rivers—the river Ouse, the Derwent (72 miles), Swale (71 miles), Ure (61 miles), Wharfe (75 miles), Nidd (55 miles), &c. These are all good, pure rivers, with fine mountain streams, and extending over thousands of square miles, and do not produce salmon worth *one thousand pounds* a year, and are as capable of being cultivated and rendered productive, as our own river was, when we purchased it, and commenced breeding and protecting the fish; but from neglect and the erection of mill weirs, they have been reduced to their present deplorable and unproductive condition. If you will read the evidence taken by the Commissioners, 1861, you will see that these Yorkshire rivers only produced a rental of about *one hundred and twenty-eight pounds.* The river Trent and its tributaries, about 500 miles in length, is in a similar condition to the Yorkshire rivers, caused by obstructions from mill weirs, navigation weirs, and neglect.

WHAT HAS BEEN DONE FOR THE THAMES AND OTHER WATERS.

Thus much, then, for Huningue, Scotland, and Ireland. We at home have not in the meantime been idle. Our noble Thames has not been neglected, for there are now in full * work at Hampton, near Hampton Court, two sets of hatching boxes, both crowded with young fish and eggs. One of

* I fear most of the fish are now (May) turned out into the river, but the boxes still remain.

these has been entirely planned as to details and erected in his greenhouse solely at the private expense of Stephen Ponder, Esq., of Hampton, without whose persevering and painstaking energy pisciculture in the Thames would probably have come to nothing, and to whom therefore too much public praise cannot be accorded. The other apparatus consists of boxes placed out of doors, in a meadow near the Thames, the water being supplied from the "Christian spring." The "Thames Angling Preservation Society" (who are doing their best to preserve our noble river from London-bridge to Staines'-bridge, to afford sport and recreation to the angler, and also to provide a delicacy for the table,) are endeavouring to stock their waters for the sake of their subscribers and the public in general,* for they have appointed a fish-culture committee of which I have the honour to be one of the members, and for the last three years we have been hatching and turning fish into the Thames, both from the out-door boxes and also Mr. Ponder's apparatus. In order that the reader shall see the latest results, I give from official returns the results of the fish-hatching of the season ending May, 1863 :—

NUMBER OF FISH TURNED OUT INTO THE THAMES.

Rhine Salmon. . .	6000
English Trout. . .	22000
French Trout. . .	2000
Ombre Chevalier (Charr).	3000
Grayling. . . .	2000
In all	35,000

* Anglers in the Thames should recollect this, and by their subscriptions enable the Society to carry out fish hatching next year even, it is hoped, on a larger scale than this year.

A few observations on this list. The salmon were presented in the form of ova by the ever-liberal M. Coumes on the part of the French government. This gentleman visited the Hampton fish-hatching works with me, and he was pleased to express his high approval of what he saw and heard. He has further shown his approval practically by the salmon ova he has sent, as he is most anxious that the attempt to restore salmon to the Thames should be persevered with.

Both Mr. Ponder and myself have often been laughed at for our experiments, and many a friendly chat we have had over the matter. The argument used by objectors has been, "Why, your salmon will never come back again."

My answer invariably has been, "No, they

will certainly never come back again, if they are never put in." * It is far from impossible, nay it is even probable, that they *will* come back when the new sewers are in operation, and the Thames water is made considerably purer than it is now. Besides this, it must be recollected, that salmon remain several months in the river before they go down to the sea, and if we continue to turn them down every year, some of them will be in a fit state to run down to the sea and come back again when this new drainage is in operation. Anyhow, they will be caught as young fish, and this week (May 8th) I hear that "skeggers" (the name applied, in former days, to young salmon) in the Thames have been

* We can turn young salmon into the Thames at the rate of about four a penny.

caught by the fly at Sunbury. I hope all Thames anglers will immediately return any fish they catch that may be a young salmon or trout. Anyhow, it is very delightful to one's ears to hear even the long extinct word "skeggers" again passing from mouth to mouth on the banks of our noble river. When shall we hear of "strikes," *i.e.* salmon after they have spawned, being found in the Thames? * The time was, and this no more

* The following is a record of the last salmon caught at Windsor. He was caught by one Finmore, an ancient fisherman of the place. I quote from my "Curiosities of Natural History."

"Nearly fifty years have passed since the last salmon at Windsor became a victim to the cupidity of man. This poor fish had a favourite hole near Surley Hall, about two miles above Windsor, which was at last found out and his destruction determined upon. Accordingly, one day the hole was surrounded with nets on every side, and the fishermen made sure of their prey; but they were mistaken. The salmon discovered suddenly that there was treachery, and, like a brave and wise fish, he made a jump, not into the net—he was too knowing for than sixty years ago, when the salmon-fishers drew their nets at the village of Barnes; where they covered the shingle with shining fish, and sent them off in a tax-cart to market, caught not eight miles from London-bridge. Shall we ever live to see this again?

As regards trout in the Thames. The ova from which these fish were hatched has been obtained, by the kindness of owners of

that—but right over it, escaping triumphant, for a time at least.

"Some days afterwards he returned home to his hole: the nets were again put round him: but this time, on to the cork-lines of the nets which were in the water was fastened a net which remained suspended in the air by a string. Again the salmon made a run and a jump; he got well over the net in the water, but fell, of course, into the net suspended in the air. He died an inglorious death, but his remains were honoured by becoming 'a dainty dish to set before a king,' for he was taken to the king, then residing at Virginia Water, who gave the lucky netter a guinea a pound for his fish: twenty guineas for the last Thames salmon."

fisheries, from Whitchurch and Overton in Hants, also from Godalming and Wycombe. The young fish, both French and English, have been turned into the Thames at Sutton, Hampton, Sunbury, Walton, Halliford, and Staines; we hope that as they grow older they will prove to have "biting" powers.

Anglers will know what a difficult matter it is to catch a Thames trout. They are generally heavy fish,* and the few fish that remain in the river require masters of the art of angling to entice them to "a run." The haunt of a big trout in the Thames is immediately marked like the haunt of the finest stag in a deer forest, and there is as

* I now show a life-size water-colour drawing of a huge trout in magnificent condition, the property of that most successful trout-fisherman, my friend J. Gould, Esq., F.R.S. A trout of 15 lb. has been caught this week at Sunbury.

much rivalry to catch him with the spinning as there is to bring down the stag with the rifle. The fish being so often "tried for," becomes amazingly cunning.

If we listen to a lecture from a learned professor, upon the brains of animals, he will point out the human brain as being at the highest end of the scale, the brain of the fish at the lowest. Holding up the brain of a trout beautifully prepared in spirits of wine, he will say, "There, gentlemen, is an example of a badly developed brain. The creature to which it belonged is of a low order of intellect." Yet the next day, if we look over a Thames weir, we may behold the same learned but sportless professor puzzling his well-developed brain to catch the creature which but yesterday he was asserting had so little brains. The brain of the fish is quite sufficient to keep him off the professor's hook, angle he never so wisely. There is a story told of a trout at Hampton, which is of a fabulous weight. This fish has been so often angled for, that he is said not only to recognise a spinning bait the instant it passes over his house, but that from long experience he even knows who made the tackle.

As regards the ombre chevalier, or charr, living in the Thames, it has been stated, upon good authority, that the ombre chevalier resides only in lakes and very deep calm waters; but we were assured by M. Coumes, at his visit to Hampton, that this fish has been introduced with success in the rivers of France, and that he considered that the Thames would prove equally suitable to it.

Desirous that the important process of fish-hatching should be made known to country gentlemen and owners of salmon and trout fisheries, I obtained the permission of the editor of "The Field" to place my apparatus in the window of his office in the Strand, where it has remained since January last. My labours in this respect have been amply repaid, not only by the general public interest excited in watching the operation, but also by the visits and anxious inquiries of many influential gentlemen and proprietors of fisheries; nay, what is still better, six or seven of my visitors have even fish-hatching boxes actually at work on their own premises, constructed after the models which I have given them.*

* I here give a list of those who have constructed fish-

I also brought the matter under the notice of Dr. P. L. Sclater and the authorities of the Zoological Society, who devoted the entire end of their aquarium-house at the gardens to the demonstration of the science of fish-hatching. The apparatus was ably designed and arranged by A. D. Bartlett, Esq., Resident Superintendent of the gardens. A great

hatching boxes. Those marked with an * have taken the designs of their apparatus either from Mr. Ponder's establishment at Hampton, or from my boxes in "The Field" window.

*His Grace the Duke of Argyll.
*The Viscount Powerscourt.
*The Earl of Mountcharles.
*Lady Dorothy Neville.
S. Gurney, Esq., M.P.[1]
Alfred Smee, Esq.[1]
*Captain Berkeley, 2nd Life Guards.
*J. Baker, Esq., of Bayfordbury.
*J. Hibbert, Esq.
*S. Hall, Esq., of Farningham.
*J. King, Esq., Watford.

[1] These two gentlemen have hatched trout many years successfully, and have turned the young fish into the Wandle.

number of fish have been hatched out during the past few months,* and have, I trust, been the cause of amusement and instruction to the visitors. It is in this apparatus that the experiments of hatching out the ova after they have been frozen have been arranged and carefully watched by Tennant the keeper.

I have also brought, from time to time, the matter before the scientific meetings of the Society, and have been much pleased with the kind reception the notes of my observations have met with from members and visitors present. At the end of one of these meetings a laughable incident occurred to myself and the young fish. (See Appendix.)

* I fear the season has now (May) passed to see this apparatus in working order. I trust the Council will sanction the repetition of the process again towards the end of this year.

I have now given the results of my observations upon the important and useful subject of fish hatching, and trust that they may prove of some benefit to the public at large.

In this point France shows a noble example to England.

What has been done in France may surely be done in England. Many gentlemen, both in their public and private capacities, have now seen the importance of pisciculture, and have already, at the cost of a few pounds, turned a useless stream of clear running water into a vivifier of thousands of fish. I trust more will imitate them. What we require is a regular Government establishment as in France, where the art should be carried out and brought to perfection, and eggs distributed to every part of this our own favoured land; this may be done at a comparatively small expense.

The subject of our fisheries is now beginning to assume considerable importance in the national mind. Parliament has found out that it is necessary to interfere to prevent the wholesale slaughter of the salmon which is going on.* They wisely foresaw the consequences of the suicidal fishing that everywhere prevailed, and determined to deal with the evil with a strong hand, and to make a magna charta for the inhabitants of our streams. This they have done, and the consequences of protection have already begun to show good results. This is an

* See note in Appendix.

important fight—a regular ichthyomachia—a battle between man and fish :—

> The clouds have gods, and gods have eyes,
> Ye fish, ye fish, your great avengers rise.

If I have in any way contributed to your instruction, or have added to your knowledge, let the merits be given to others. Let whatever approval you may be pleased to show be accorded as a contribution to the memory of that great and good man whose portrait I rejoice to see hanging on your walls, who has so often addressed you from this very spot where I now stand, and whose honoured name I have the high privilege to bear.

APPENDIX.

TRANSFER OF SALMON TO AUSTRALIA.

Page 185.

The question of the transport of salmon to Australia is just now exciting great public interest. The Australian authorities have voted considerable sums of money towards carrying out this object, and have caused several experiments to be made, which have not met with a very satisfactory result. A new series of experiments have now been instituted, and by the kindness of my friend, J. Youl, Esq., I have been allowed to add my humble assistance in developing the theory that the only way to carry salmon to Australia will be by freezing the ova in ice, and hatching the young fish out when arrived at their destination. Through the kindness of the Editor, I am enabled to give consecutive reports of these experiments, which have from time to time appeared in "The Field," and which, as the idea is novel and the results highly satisfactory, cannot fail to be interesting. There are, I am aware, many persons who tell us that salmon can never be taken to Australia, and if they arrive there, they can never live there; anyhow, we shall see what is to be done; if it is a failure, why then it is a failure;

but if a success—what a success. We read in "The Field" as follows:—

"On Saturday, the 17th January, 1863, James A. Youl, Esq., Mr. Robert Ramsbottom, of Clitheroe, Mr. William Ramsbottom, and Mr. Thomas Johnson, were engaged during the greater portion of the day in arranging the beginning of several experiments of a somewhat novel character. Our readers are aware of the failure of the last attempt to transport salmon ova to Australia, showing that many difficulties have yet to be overcome. It would appear, from the journal of Mr. William Ramsbottom, that some salmon ova, which Mr. Youl had placed in a deal box amongst moss, and imbedded in the ice-house on board the 'Beautiful Star' (the vessel chartered), lived from March 4th to May 17th. In order to test the theory, backed by the apparent fact mentioned in the journal of Mr. Ramsbottom, Mr. Youl obtained leave from the Wenham Lake Ice Company, in the Strand, to carry out, under inspection, a series of experiments. With this view, one of the company's large ice-houses was selected, and eight small deal boxes, containing moss, charcoal, and ice, and the salmon ova, were buried amongst the ice. Some other preparations were then made, and with other boxes taken to the premises of the company in the Strand."

The boxes were left undisturbed till 3rd of March, when Mr. Youl kindly invited me to be present at the examination of the results, which he reports as follows:—

"I send you the following remarks on the state of the salmon ova placed in a refrigerator on

January 17th, and observed for the first time on March 3rd, forty-five days after being deposited; the object being, as has already been stated in 'The Field,' to test the suitability of the plan as a means of effecting the transport of salmon ova to Australia. The experiments were these:—

"First Box.—The ova in this box were packed between layers of moss, thoroughly saturated with water, and placed in an ordinary meat safe. The refrigerator was constantly supplied with ice in a separate apartment, and kept at an uniform temperature of 36°. No water or ice or anything had been added to this box, except once during the second week, when a small piece of ice was placed in the top of the box, which melted in a few hours. On being opened, the ova appeared perfectly healthy, and fewer were found dead than is generally the case in the very best breeding-boxes. Mr. Frank Buckland took a few out to try and hatch them in order to prove their vitality, and he also placed some of these ova in a bottle, with sponge intervening, in the same way that he has received ova from Huningue, to try the difference, if any, between sponge and moss in the refrigerator. A few were also given to Mr. Johnson to hatch. The box was then carefully screwed down again, and replaced under lock and key.

"Second Box.—The ova in this box were packed in wet moss, and then placed in the large ice-box in use at the Wenham Lake Ice Company's office, 140, Strand; and upon the top of this box (which was perforated with holes) ice was constantly placed. As soon as one piece melted, it was replaced, and the melted water, passing through the moss and ova, escaped through holes at the bottom of the box. Upon its being opened, the ova appeared perfectly healthy, but there were more dead ones than in the first box, occasioned perhaps by the pressure of the moss, which being constantly kept wet may have expanded, and thus occasioned more pressure than was good. The temperature in this case was about 33°. After being carefully examined, it was replaced, not to be opened again until a further lapse of thirty days.—J. YOUL.

"March 4, 1863.
"The Editor of 'The Field.'"

Mr. Youl kindly gave me some five or six of these eggs, which I placed in my hatching-boxes, but they all died. Mr. Johnson also had some eggs, and met with a better result, for he reports—

"Two hours after leaving the Wenham Lake Ice Company's offices, on the 3rd instant, I deposited the ova taken from each box in a small earthenware dish, containing moss and water, with two small jets of running water at a temperature of 46°. Before depositing the ova, I took one dead ovum from those taken from the first box. On the following morning two more from amongst the same lot. The remainder of the ova are apparently looking well. The temperature of the water varies from 40° to 46°."

We continued our observations, and on March 25th, examining again the condition of the ova in the boxes, Mr. Youl writes:—

"Sir,—Yesterday, the two boxes of salmon ova which had been opened and looked at on the 3rd instant, and referred to in your journal of the 7th, were again examined by Mr. Buckland, Mr. Marcroft Johnson, myself, and other gentlemen who take an interest in the experiment, and the ova found to be in perfect health. They had been fifty-nine days in the refrigerator, and the ice-box; at a temperature of 34° in the former, and 33° in the latter. A few were taken out and given to Mr. Buckland and Mr. Johnson to test their vitality by hatching them in the usual way.—March 28th.

"After having replaced these boxes, we went to the ice-vaults of the Wenham Lake Ice Company, at Blackfriars, and exhumed one of the boxes containing ova that had been buried (as many persons prognosticated, in their icy graves) on the 17th of January last. I cannot describe the anxiety of all present to get a first sight of these ova, or the pleasure visible on every countenance to find as the moss (shrouds, as many expected) was removed, our little friends alive and perfectly healthy. Mutual congratulations and shaking of hands ensued. Magnifying glasses were produced, and the ova most carefully examined, to ascertain if our first impressions were true. 'All right!' exclaimed the indefatigable Buckland, 'all right!'

"Some of the ova were then given to Mr. Johnson, and the exhumed box with the remainder carried off in triumph by Mr. Buckland, to test their vitality by endeavouring to hatch them.

"Some small pieces of ice which I had placed on the top of the moss inside the box, with the idea that they would melt, and thus give a small supply of water to the ova, were found in the same state as when deposited—a proof that the temperature of the ova could never have exceeded 32°, or these pieces of ice would have melted away.

"The six remaining boxes were again covered with blocks of ice, with the intention of examining one at intervals of twenty or thirty days, to learn if the ova can be kept alive in an ice-house a sufficient length of time to reach Tasmania, and then be taken out at the end of the voyage and hatched in the stream of water in the colony.—James A. Youl.

"Waratah House, Clapham Park, March 26."

The next week I was enabled to record the following satisfactory results:—

"It will be remembered that, in the last 'Field,' Mr. Youl reported the result of the exhumation from a dense mass of ice blocks in the vaults of the Wenham Lake Ice Company of a box containing newly-impregnated salmon ova, which had been buried from January 17th to March 25th—in all sixty-eight days. He kindly consigned some of these to myself, as well as to Mr. Johnson. When first taken from the ice they were apparently alive; but, in order to make the experiment quite certain, Tennant, the keeper of the Zoological Gardens, was in attendance, and took them up immediately to place them in the admirable hatching apparatus constructed by the society; the object being to ascertain for Mr. Youl and our Australian friends whether they would ever hatch out after such a long period of freezing. The following is Tennant's report received by me this morning, April 2nd, of the state of these eggs, and all must rejoice to see that the experiment so far is highly encouraging and satisfactory.—F. Buckland."

"*Salmon Eggs taken from the Wells of the Wenham Lake Ice Company, after being Deposited in the Ice Fifty-nine Days.*

"March 25.—Forty-five of the eggs I put in the hatching apparatus *two* hours after they were taken from the wells, the temperature of the water 56°.

"March 26.—Ten were turned quite white, and dead, of course, although at the time they were taken from the box they looked alive.

"March 27.—Five more were dead.

"March 29.—Two dead. The remaining twenty-eight I believe to be doing well, as they look quite clear and healthy.

"The remainder of the eggs, twenty-eight in number, I left in the box until next morning (March 26). I put them in a separate box, the temperature of the water being 48°. Next day eight were dead.

"March 31.—Two more dead. The remainder are *now all right.* Mr. Youl and Mr. Buckland gave me six eggs which had been in the refrigerator at a temperature of 34°, fifty-nine days; when I got to the gardens, one was dead; the others, this day, April 2, are all well.—JAMES TENNANT.

"Fish House, Zoological Gardens, Regent's Park,
April 4."

On the 25th of April, I gave the following report:—

"Sir,—Your readers will, I am sure, be as much pleased as Mr. Youl, myself, and other gentlemen interested in these experiments are, at the following report of how the eggs have behaved themselves after they have been taken from their long imprisonment in the ice. They have been taken every care of by Tennant, the keeper of the Aquarium-house, Zoological Gardens, who reports as follows:—

"'On March 25th, I received six salmon eggs which had been fifty-nine days in the refrigerator of the Wenham Lake Ice Company, in the Strand.

"'On April 14th, *two* of these hatched out, the other four were bad.

"'On March 25th, I received seventy-five eggs, which had been buried deep in a block of ice in the ice-wells fifty-nine days. These began to hatch out on the 18th of April, and finished hatching on the 21st of April. Out of this lot fifty-two eggs were bad, but the remaining twenty-three hatched out properly, and are now strong and lively, and still remain in the place where they were born.

"'On April 17th, the day of Mr. Buckland's lecture, Mr. Youl gave me a box which contained thirty-five salmon eggs, that had been buried in the ice-wells *ninety days*. I placed them in the hatching-box next morning, at a temperature of 50°; five of the eggs are bad, but in most of the others the eyes are fully developed.—J. TENNANT, Fish-house, Zoological Gardens, April 22nd.'

"On May 9th, Tennant reports of these eggs: some began to hatch out on the 28th of April, and finished hatching May 6th—twenty-six young ones and nine bad eggs. The young fish are not so large as those whose incubation has not been retarded by freezing, but still they are very lively little fish.

"These results, therefore, especially the last, are most encouraging, and we fully hope that next season the actual experiment of sending the eggs to Australia, in a fast-sailing ship, packed in ice, according to the experience now gained, will be attempted. "F. T. BUCKLAND."

SALMON OVA IN ICE.

"Sir,—Will you be pleased to insert the inclosed letter received by me this morning? Mr. Ramsbottom, the writer, is the person whom I sent out in charge of the experiment in the 'Beautiful Star,' and has been sent home by the government of Tasmania to learn all he can previous to going out in charge of another attempt to be made next year to introduce salmon to the rivers of that colony.

"The salmon ova to which he alludes were taken from a pair of fish by his father, and brought up to London five days afterwards, and placed by me in wet moss inclosed in a small box, and then deposited in the ice-vaults of the Wenham Lake Ice Company, from which they were taken after being buried ninety days. The result of this experiment is of the most interesting character. Notice: the ova were taken at Clitheroe, brought up to London, exposed to railway and cab travelling, then put in ice for ninety days at a temperature never exceeding 32°; taken out egg by egg, placed in a bottle of water, taken back to Clitheroe, and now in a fair way (the most of them) to become young fish, if not 30lb. salmon.

"JAMES A. YOUL.

"Waratah House, Clapham Park, April 22."

"Clitheroe, Lancashire, April 22.

"Dear Sir,—I arrived safe here on Saturday afternoon, and I am pleased to say that I only lost four ova from leaving the Wenham Lake ice-house to reaching home; two have died since; but the rest are looking well.

"We can see that about twenty of the ova have young fish formed in them, and father thinks they are about half hatched. The rest, fourteen in number, keep their transparency, but do not appear that they ever will have young fish in them (as we cannot see anything formed in the eggs at all). We are not much surprised at this, it being often the case before. I would like the little box which I brought up at first (the one with boiled moss) to remain in the ice-chamber until the ova is 150 days old, and then to have the small box packed in a larger one with ice, and sent here by rail for hatching, if the ova should at that time be living.—I remain, yours, most obediently,

"W. Ramsbottom.

"To J. A. Youl, Esq., Waratah House,
Clapham Park, London."

It is, therefore, quite evident from these experiments, that if salmon are ever to be transported to Australia, it will be done by freezing the ova in ice, and afterwards developing the egg into the fish on its arrival in Australia. Every one will grant that it is a most difficult undertaking, but *that* is no reason why we should not make the attempt. Who knows what results may ensue to our colonies if this plan be carried out—as it will be—with perseverance and energy?

I understand from Mr. Youl that R. Cameron, Esq., who sends cargoes of ice from New York to Melbourne, for commercial purposes, has offered to bury the boxes of salmon ova among the blocks of ice in his ships. There are plenty of salmon ova to be obtained near Quebec, and Mr. Nettle, Superintendent of Fisheries at Quebec, has offered to procure and pack them for the experiment.

On the 13th of May Mr. Youl, Mr. E. Wilson, and myself examined some ova that had been 120 days in the ice. Though some were dead, the greater part were alive, and are now placed in hatching boxes. The result cannot be known before this book is published, but the appearance of the ova promises well.

REPORT BY M. COUMES ON THE FISHERIES OF FRANCE.

Page 190.

The valuable report of the government engineer-in-chief of the works of the Rhine, M. Coumes, contains an account of the system of artificial propagation, carried on by the French Government successfully for a period of ten years. The report forms a book of 143 pages, from which the following information has been collected.

The French Government has been engaged in discovering and maturing the utility of pisciculture; and a report was made in 1850, showing the advantages to be derived from artificial propagation, previously to which experiments had been made at the College of France. M. Coste then demonstrated that the re-stocking of the rivers of France with fish, and the acclimatisation of foreign species, was a work of public utility, and proposed to establish the institution at Huningue, near Basle, and which was commenced on the 5th of August, 1852.

The capabilities and influence of this establishment have opened a new field of enterprise on a large scale, and, promoted by Government, was placed under the State administration of the roads and bridges, with the view of increasing the supply of food to the people.

On the 5th of October, 1852, the arrangement of the works at Huningue was agreed upon by Messrs. Coste and Berthot and Detzen, upon a surface of 35 hectares (about 70 statute acres), with an abundant supply of spring water, at a temperature of 10° centigrade, with an additional supply from other streams.

The experience derived in 1853 and 1854 confirmed the preceding experiments, both with regard to artificial propagation and the transport of ova.

In 1854, suitable buildings were erected, with ponds and other requisites, the cost of which was estimated at 154,000 francs. Ponds were made for the reception of each species of fish to be propagated for re-stocking the rivers and canals, and for the supply of individuals. M. Coste was instructed to make further experiments, and to publish annual reports upon the collection and distribution of the ova, and as to the results obtained at the College of France.

The total outlay in the construction of ponds, conduits, buildings, and apparatus, from 1852 to

1862, amounts to 265,186 francs, or say 10,607*l.* The object in view was to stock the rivers with fish by the introduction of ova and young fry of the best kinds, and those of rapid growth—salmon, trout, ombre chevalier, and fera, heuch, alose, and sturgeon, the sterlet, and silure. The operations on such species of fish as spawned in winter succeeded at once, whilst great difficulties attended the impregnation and transport of the ova of other kinds that spawned in the spring and summer.

The ova have been principally collected in Switzerland and Germany, and procured at various seasons with great care and by competent men employed for the purpose. On their arrival at Huningue they are examined, and the quantity ascertained by means of small stamped measures, according to the kinds of fish and the size of the ova, the spoiled ova being separated from the sound, and the whole is then carefully recorded; the sound ova being carefully deposited for incubation in separate compartments, and such as may become addled are daily abstracted from the boxes; and after two or three weeks those that remain in a healthy condition are selected, packed up in wet moss, and inclosed in wood cases, and are forwarded to various districts by the Government free of any expense. The ova are given away for restocking the waters, but the parties who receive packets of ova are required to give detailed accounts of the success of their previous operations before a second supply be granted to them, the demand for ova having always been greater than the means of supplying it.

The expenses of conducting the establishment,

in which is included all the men employed, the maintenance of the building, the manipulation of the fish, carriage, packing, travelling expenses in collecting the ova, purchase of ova, salaries, &c., including the entire operations from 1853 to 1862, amounts to 347,186 francs, or say 13,887*l.*; the average annual expenses during the past four years have been 55,000 francs, or say 2200*l.*

The ova are collected and impregnated at remote places, they are then conveyed to Huningue and partly hatched; after which they are packed, forwarded, and distributed to such rivers as may require a supply. For the past two years the establishment has also distributed young fry by way of experiment, but this mode cannot be greatly extended, owing to the increased expense and difficulty of transit.

The following tabular statements of the result of operations are interesting, as they show the various kinds of fish that have been artificially propagated in the season of 1861:—

1*st.*—*Salmon Trout, Lake Trout, Rhine Salmon, Ombre Chevalier.*	Ova.		Total.
Ova collected of the above species . .		. . . . . .	6,382,900
Ova lost and died from the time of collection to the time when sent away from the establishment	2,602,400	= 41 per cent.	
Ova forwarded to various places, sound .	3,360,000	= 53 per cent.	
Ova hatched at the establishment . .	420,500	= 6 per cent.	
Carry forward,	6,382,900		6,382,900

	Ova.		Total.
2nd.—Danube Salmon (heuch).			
Brought forward,	6,382,900		6,382,900
Ova collected of heuch .		. . . . . .	43,500
Ova lost and died as above	35,450	= 81 per cent.	
Ova forwarded to various places . . .	2,000	= 5 per cent.	
Ova hatched at the establishment . .	6,050	= 14 per cent.	
3rd.—Ombre.			
Ova collected		. . . . . .	1,028,000
Ova lost and died as above	550,500	= 54 per cent.	
Ova forwarded, sound	251,500	= 24 per cent.	
Ova hatched at the establishment . .	221,000	= 22 per cent.	
4th.—Fera.			
Ova collected as above		. . . . . .	11,995,000
Ova lost and died as above	12,000		
Ova forwarded to various rivers, &c., sound	9,519,000	= 80 per cent.	
Ova hatched at the establishment . . .	2,464,000	= 20 per cent.	
Total	16,244,050		19,449,400

The result of the last year's propagation shows that from 19,449,400 of the ova collected, no less than 16,244,050, after having been partially hatched for a period of two or three weeks, were forwarded in a sound state to upwards of 238 different places, to be deposited and incubated in various waters. It is also stated that of the quantity sent 88 to 92 per cent. had arrived in a sound state at the places of destination. The ova were sent to sixty-three French departments and to eleven foreign countries in 1861.

In conclusion the report states :—"The results

relative to the transport and the hatching of the ova, as well as to the production of fry, are very satisfactory; they may be approximately estimated at one-third of living fish, in proportion to the quantity of ova collected; and the increase of fish in the rivers and ponds has been confirmed by numerous testimonies, and the number of pisci-cultural associations has rapidly increased."

The results are very elaborately shown in fourteen tabular statements prepared with great minuteness (we only take the last year's returns), and from these it appears that 19,449,400 ova had been collected, of eight different species of fish, at a cost of 2200*l.* If we estimate thirty-six ova to have cost one penny, this quantity would amount to 2251*l.* 1*s.* 9*d.* The report states that "they may be approximately estimated at one-third as living fish," thus producing twelve living fish for one penny, or 6,483,133 living fish for the sum of 2200*l.*, and introduced into the various rivers and waters of France last year; that is, if in England we take 300,000 salmon ova to have been collected at thirty-six for a penny, the cost would be 34*l.* 14*s.* 5*d.*, at a similar rate to those produced in France; and, taking one-third to be living fish, the result should be an increase of 100,000 young salmon, or twelve for a penny.

With such statements before us, and after a period of ten years' experience, it would be difficult to arrive at any other conclusion than that the experiments had proved, as they are stated to have been, "very satisfactory."

M. Coumes states further, that the propagation of Rhine salmon (*Salar*), common trout, salmon trout, lake trout, and ombre chevalier, is the easiest; the results are very certain. The loss of ova from these kinds has varied from 30 to 34 and 41 per cent. in the last three years, and that this loss is only half of what it had been in previous years, as the men are more careful and understand the collection and manipulation better.

The Danube salmon (heuch) is very difficult to propagate; it has to be brought a great distance, and the loss of ova has been as much as 89, 93, and 81 per cent., arising from circumstances that are unknown. They are easily hatched, but the young fry die in a month after coming to life, and they have not yet discovered the reason why they are so delicate, but they require a different mode of treatment before they become acclimatised. M. Coumes sent me 1000 ova of these fish, April 4th, 1863. I regret to say they were badly packed, and most of them had hatched out in the bottles, and were therefore dead. The ombre chevalier is more easily propagated than the heuch, and can be reared in small basins of three feet in depth of water, and they live and do well.

The fera fish, when fully grown, is about twelve inches in length; each fish produces a very large quantity of eggs (10,000 to 20,000); but, as it is very small, the quantity is unknown. They are caught in the night—it is called the herring of the lakes. The young fish on leaving the egg is so small that it can scarcely be seen in the water, and can penetrate the smallest openings; and in this way it escapes from the boxes and places where it may have been hatched, so that the number of fish cannot be correctly ascertained, but he states that it is immensely prolific. The ova have been sent to stock great numbers of lakes and rivers in France, and in a few years the results may be ascertained. The fishermen have caught some fera in the Rhine, near Huningue, which must have escaped from the ponds. The ova are brought from Bavaria and Switzerland, where this fish lives only in deep waters, and only frequents the borders of the lake to deposit its spawn.

The French Government intend to extend the present system of pisciculture, to improve the fishery laws, to encourage the cultivation of fish wherever parties may be inclined, and to introduce the best kinds where fish do not at present exist. In many rivers where trout and salmon were unknown, they are now to be found in great abundance since the ova have been sent to them. M. Coumes states that the present laws allow any person to catch fish at all seasons with a rod and line, except in the breeding season; but as different kinds of fish breed at different seasons, so the men fish at all seasons of the year with a rod and line; but no one is allowed to fish with a net unless he pays a rent to Government. No person can fish in private waters, and if he does so without consent he may be punished; but in public waters the rent varies from 1*l.* to 4*l.* a year; the size of the mesh of the net is fixed by Government according to the kind of fish to be caught, and is made so large that the small fish escape. The rivers are divided like farms, so that each fisherman cannot interfere with any other.

The silure fish is found in the lakes of Bavaria: it is a fresh water fish; it varies in length from four feet to six feet, and weighs 30lb. to 40lb. It is found in deep lakes, is difficult to catch, but very good to eat.

The sterlet is a Russian fish, and is found in the rivers of the Baltic and in Prussia. It is the most esteemed fish as food in all Russia. It is about eighteen inches in length, and weighs 2lb. or 3lb.

The alose fish is found in France and all over Europe: it is from one to two feet in length, and weighs 1lb. to 2lb. In some rivers it is good to eat, and in others it is not good food. In the river Loire it is very good, but when caught in the Rhine it is not eatable.

THOMAS ASHWORTH.

August 25, 1862.

REPORT OF PROCEEDINGS AT STORMONTFIELD.

Page 201.

"Peter of the Pool" thus writes to the Editor of "The Field":—

"We began the operation of spawning on the 11th of November last, and finished on the 2nd of December. On the 11th only a few males were found ripe, but all the fish hauled that day were found in a state far towards spawning. We then tried it on the 13th, when we got 10,000 ova, and every alternate day thereafter more or less, till our boxes were completely filled, on the 2nd December. During that time we netted 119 salmon and 231 grilse, out of which eighteen salmon and twenty-two grilse were found to be quite mature, and they were successfully manipulated, and the produce are now alive in the boxes. We cannot say what proportion of the above were male and female fish, as the milt of one male was used for the ova of two or three females. But the results in living fish show that the operations were successfully performed.

"It will be observed that towards the end of our operations the fish were getting fast to maturity. From eighteen salmon and twenty-two grilse we had filled our breeding-boxes with 275,000 ova. Immediately after our ponds were filled the rivers came out in great floods, which dispersed the salmon, and, it is feared that, as these floods continue till the end of December, the fine appearance of fish would come to little account when left to all the contingencies of spawning in the rivers. The 310 fish not spawned would all be ripe within ten days, so that from those left to their natural course there would not have been so many fecundated eggs from the 310 as we have in the breeding-boxes from the forty fish. All these fish were caught on one ford where the Almond joins the Tay. The Almond is a small river where only breeding fish go, and not a clean salmon is got in it during the fishing season. It is only when the river is in flood that the fish when breeding can enter, and it was only about the middle of December last year when they did so. After spawning in the Almond they have many perils to encounter, and few of the fry can get down to the Tay by the natural channel of the river, but are forced to come down by an aqueduct which supplies a number of mills between the river and Perth, and which in summer takes in the whole stream. Therefore al spawn in the Almond comes to very poor account. Had we a field for it we could have planted the whole of the produce as at Stormontfield. But our works are on a small scale only, having room for 300,000; and having only one feeding pond, we can only fill our boxes once in the two years, because the first year's fish would devour the young of the second if allowed to go among them. This season thirty of the boxes were so leaky by decay of the wood that we put nothing in them.

"Of the 275,000 ova in our boxes, the whole are now quick and bursting into life, a great many of them are already hatched, and the others are very healthy, and the young fish may clearly be seen in them, and are bursting the shell daily. In consequence of the fine open winter, the eggs have hatched in our ponds in 115 days, and have done so corresponding to the days on which the eggs were deposited. Thus the eggs on the 13th of November have hatched on the 8th of March, and have continued doing so in the corresponding days. In former seasons they have taken from 130 to 140 days, according to the temperature of the water. In spring water flowing from the rock in winter, where the temperature is always equal, I have known them to hatch in about sixty days."

INGENIOUS EXPERIMENT WITH THE FRESH-WATER CADDIS.

Page 50.

"My efforts to promote the practical application of observed facts of natural history during the delivery of my lecture on 'Fish Hatching,' at the Royal Institution, have been so handsomely and flatteringly mentioned in your columns, that I cannot refrain from giving more details about one of the specimens I placed upon the table to illustrate my subject, and this because it was the handiwork of a lady, or, rather, it was the idea of a lady carried out by representatives of a humble class of insects.

"Everybody knows the humble caddis worm, that neglected but really interesting creature which is found so plentifully in ponds and stagnant ditches. If you will examine one of them you will find that the creature has surrounded his body and built for himself a movable house—like the gipsy's moving caravan—of sticks, stones, water-shells—in fact, any material he could get hold of; just as we ourselves at Brighton build houses and walls of flints, or in London dig up the London clay (as it is called by geologists), and, having baked it into bricks, build our houses of the materials nearest at hand. If we want further illustrations, look, reader, at the substance with which your own house is built. If you are at Bath, you will find it is built of Bath stone; if at Oxford, of oolite; if in Cornwall, of granite, and so on. Just in the same way the caddis, living in a ditch, builds his house of the materials of which the bottom of the ditch is formed.

"Now, an ingenious-minded, observant, and clever-fingered young lady, Miss Smee—daughter of Alfred Smee, Esq., whose practical and clever researches in science are so well known—reasoned that if the caddis were taken out of the house which he had formed from the materials he found at the bottom of the Wandle, and given materials wherewith to build a new house, he would rather use these, whatever they might happen to be, than have no house at all. She therefore set to work, and put the caddis to work also; for, having despoiled him of his house, she gave him other materials which he might use or leave alone as he chose. The consequence of her most interesting experiments was that she has been enabled to show a glass case, neatly fitted up, containing specimens of the most curious caddis-houses that have ever been seen by the naturalist. In this collection we find caddis-houses made of the following most un-caddis-like materials, viz., bits of glass, both white and coloured, of coral, of amethyst, onyx, cairngorm, gold, silver, brass, and numerous other materials which the ingenuity of Miss Smee had devised, forming altogether a remarkable example of how human intelligence can cause the instinct of minor creatures to work for man, according to its own design. The caddis refused to use bits of coal, brick, or slate; also tin, lead, or copper. Miss Smee observed that the greatest number of houses that a caddis would build was five, and that every house they formed was more and more fragile. They cement the bits of the material they are *obliged* to use together in a most ingenious way, by means of a secretion from the mouth, and it is curious to see them adapting the bits into the places which they best fit, just as we see a labourer building a wall of rough chalk flint. During their hard labours the caddis worms were fed with raw meat, house-flies, &c.

"It is curious to observe that, if the caddis lives in a rapid stream, he builds himself a heavy house, as though aware that, if he did not do so, he and his house together would be swept away by the stream. But in a stagnant stream, his house is light, for he does not want the weight to keep himself down; so that there may be said to be laziness in the caddis family as well as in our noble selves.

"Miss Smee's preparations have been exhibited at the Zoological Society, and a paper read upon the subject by the eminent naturalist, Dr. John Edward Gray, of the British Museum, who was pleased to pay a high compliment to Miss Smee's ingenuity in devising and cleverness in carrying out her experiments.

"FRANK BUCKLAND.
"May 2, 1862."

"The Editress of
'The Queen,' 'The Lady's Newspaper,'
346, Strand, W.C."

TRANSPORT OF LIVE SALMON.

Page 197.

Mr. Ashworth tells me, that on 20th December, 1862, he transported forty spawning salmon twenty-three miles. He placed them in a large tub, and then put the tub in an ordinary springless cart, with wisps of straw between the tub and the cart and the splashing about from the jolting of the cart, caused the water to be well aerated, &c. Fresh was added at every opportunity. The expense was very slight. The fish arrived at their destination as lively as when they started, and have deposited the spawn, thus re-peopling a vast tract of water. It should be recollected that fish carry better in cold than hot weather.

HOW TO TAKE THE OVA FROM THE FISH.

Page 83.

All fish hatching experiments will, of course, be useless, unless the ova of the fish can be obtained in a fit state to develop themselves in the hatching boxes. I have already explained that the eggs of the fish are commonly called the "hard roe;" *soft* roe, is the milt. It is by the contact of the milt with the ova that life is imparted to what otherwise would be simply a mass of inert albumen. The object in view, therefore, is to place the milt and the ova in such a position that the one shall have free access to and vivify the other.

I have several times had an opportunity of performing the operation, which, after all, is simple enough, and which M. Coste so aptly terms "*Pro cédés de fécondation artificielle;*" and I therefore give the following directions, derived from my own experience, and trust that they may be found to be sufficiently explicit; should they not, I shall be glad to explain any difficulties the reader may meet with, if he will communicate with me. My experience extends only to trout, but the same rules apply also to salmon. See Mr. Ashworth's book for instructions as applied to these fish.

1st. Have your hatching apparatus in perfect order to receive the eggs, when you bring them home from the river side.

2nd. Be on the look-out for several weeks beforehand for information where and when the fish will be "at hill," *i.e.*, spawning on their natural beds in the river, and be sure have proper *written* authority from the owner of the fisheries to allow you to proceed with your operations.*

3rd. When you know the fish are "at hill," proceed to the river-side with the nets and a large shallow tub or bucket, or other convenient vessel to contain for a few minutes the fish as caught; also bring with you a vessel, such as a small washing-tub, in which to impregnate the ova. It should be flat-bottomed, to prevent the eggs being crowded one upon the other; and, also, do not forget the bottles, tin (milk or fish bait) cans, in which you are about to carry home the eggs.

4th. When the fish are caught, examine them one

* Trout spawn at different periods in different rivers, from about September to February—the Wandle is the latest river near London. Salmon spawn in the winter months; grayling, generally speaking, at the end of April or beginning of May.

by one. If the ova of the female are ripe, they will pour out from the abdomen at the slightest pressure of the hand. Handle the fish gently. If the milt of the male be ripe, it will also, upon slight pressure, *be observed to flow out like thin milk.*

5th. Place your captured fish in the large tubs or buckets that you may select for them till you are quite ready to take the spawn. It is not a bad plan to catch your fish some few days before they go to hill, and confine them in some suitable and healthy, roomy place (but not boxes or baskets), whence you can take them out from time to time with a landing net, and, if ripe, proceed to operate on them immediately.

6th. Fill your small tub (or tin bowl) three parts full with clean cold water.

7th. Examine the fish in the tub one by one, and return the unripe fish to the river or reservoir.

8th. Take a female fish that is ripe; hold her head with your left hand; get an assistant to steady the tail; gently submerge the lower part of the body into your small bowl; then gently and carefully pass your right hand downwards from the head to the tail, the thumb and forefinger gently compressing the abdomen, the other fingers following behind as assistants. You should also slightly bend the fish backwards, in a bow-shaped form. If the eggs are quite ripe, you will see in an instant that they all pour out into the water, following each other in a most rapid succession, reminding us exactly of shot running out of a shot-belt, when loading a gun. Continue your downward pressure as long as the eggs continue to come out. If you find the eggs do not come out *quite* easily, give the tail of the fish a *gentle* shake, to loosen those eggs that still remain in the abdomen; but recollect if you use *force*, you will spoil the experiment. The eggs *must* run out quite freely.

9th. The eggs being collected at the bottom of the vessel, take a male fish. Make pressure on the abdomen, in the same way as has been done to the female. If the melt is ripe, it will instantly discolour the water, making it of a cream, or rather milk-white appearance. Stir the eggs and milt gently together, and leave them quiet for three or four minutes, pour off the milk-coloured water, and gently add fresh water, till the eggs appear quite clear again.* If this has been properly and carefully done, the eggs have been thoroughly impregnated. Place the eggs in the vessel by means of which you intend to take them to the hatching apparatus, and carry them in your hand, without shaking. If you remain out a night, stand the bottle or can with the eggs in a tub of cold water.

As regards the number of males to females, be sure to obtain sufficient males before you begin to operate. The milt of one male will impregnate the ova of many females; but it is not wise to get the eggs from a female, and then have no milt to place with them. You can impregnate one lot of eggs with a male, place him back into the temporary reservoir, and use him for other lots of eggs.

* Return the fish you have spawned to the river; if you have been neat-handed they will be none the worse for the operation.

I hope by next September or October to be able to inform my readers where they will be able to get trout and salmon ova ready for their boxes.

In order to understand what actually happens during the curious and instantaneous act of fecundation, I have examined the milt under the microscope, taken at the moment from the fish. What appears like milk to the naked eye is, in fact, one living mass, containing myriads and myriads of those mysterious creatures called by physiologists spermatozoa. Each seems endowed with independent power of motion, and, I almost think, volition. Under the microscope they are seen to hurry and push about, as if in search of something on to which they may attach themselves; that something is the ovum; but having found it, they attach themselves, and, I believe, actually enter into its substance.

OUT-DOOR APPARATUS.

Page 83.

The accompanying engraving will give the reader an idea of how an out-door apparatus may be constructed (see page 83). The plan of it was kindly given to my friend Mr. Ashworth, as giving an idea of the method he has adopted to hatch so many thousands of salmon. It will be seen that the boxes, which are 6 feet long, by 12 inches wide, and 7 inches deep, are placed one above another, so that the water shall fall from the outflow of the one into the inflow of the next. The inflow from the main stream must, of course, be regulated by a hatchway (where the man is working with the fish-kettle and net), and be guarded by perforated

OUT-DOOR APPARATUS.

zinc, &c. It may be also, if naturally not very clear, filtered through gravel, charcoal, &c.; and the top box may be devoted to this service. It is not necessary that the boxes should be placed on the side of a hill, as represented in the drawing; but still they should be placed one above the other, in such a manner that there should be a fall from one to the other. Nor is it absolutely necessary that the end of the upper box should rest on that immediately below it. The water may be conducted from one to the other by means of a trough or plate (with the margins turned up) of common zinc. The pond at the end of the boxes will receive the fish; but they should not be allowed to escape there till the umbilical bag is gone. The pond must not be above three or four feet deep; or if it be naturally deep, the margins must be made to slope, as the young fish like shallow water to bask, feed, and play upon. They must be fed for a time when in this pond. The boxes should have solid boards, or boards fitted with perforated zinc, made to fit their tops by means of hinges and padlocks, to keep out all intruders—biped, quadruped, or aquatic.

IN-DOOR APPARATUS.

Page 91.

As I have said in the text, the in-door is far preferable to the out-door apparatus. The accompanying drawing shows the troughs best suited for the purpose, each is fitted with a lip which conducts the water from one to the other. They can be multiplied one above the other *ad infinitum.*

The hands of the operator can be seen (No. 1) placing in the framework of glass rods (which rests upon projections in the inside of the troughs, made to receive it when in its place). The eggs should be placed upon these rods, and left to hatch out.

The lower tank (No. 2) represents the fish eggs resting upon gravel—as good, but not as pretty, a manner of treating them. The water from the tap above must be flowing incessantly with a gentle, but not rapid, stream. You should have boards made to fit over the tops of the troughs while the eggs are being developed into fish.

I am in communication with a London manufacturer as regards making these troughs, and hope that they will be obtainable at a small price by the next fish-egg season.

The tanks can be made of zinc (as mine are in "The Field" window), viz., two feet long, five inches wide, four inches deep, with one side of glass. These can be fixed by means of blocks of wood, one above the other, end over end—the same idea, on a small scale, as is given for the outdoor apparatus. If the water does not run freely from the tubes, they should be lengthened by an inch or two of india-rubber pipe fastened over them.

Fig. 3 represents what I call the "catcher," a most useful instrument for moving the eggs without touching them. Place the finger on the end of the straight part of the tube, immerse it in the water, and bring the lower end opposite the egg or impurity you wish to remove. When the finger is withdrawn the water rushes instantly into the tube, and with it the object, fish, egg, or weed you wish to withdraw. These catchers were designed

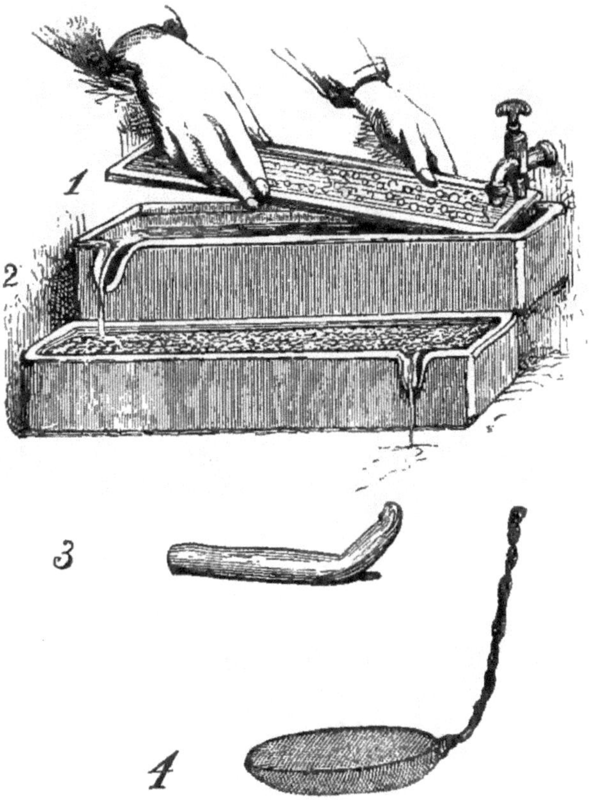

IN-DOOR APPARATUS.

[*See page opposite.*

by my friend the Rev. Cyril Page, and can be obtained of Mr. G. King, aquarium dealer, 190, Portland Road.

Fig. 4 represents a net made of common wire, and the material the Ladies call "net." It will be found useful to catch the young fish. This in-door apparatus can be fixed up almost anywhere under cover, except in a *hot* greenhouse. It will be found much easier of management than the out-door apparatus.

GRAYLING IN SCOTLAND.

Page 202.

I here give an extract from the diary of "The Field Crew on the Clyde,"* of which I formed one, written by my excellent friend, J. Lowe, Esq., "the chronicler."

"Up to a very recent period the waters of the Upper Clyde have presented nothing tempting to the angler but the trout. Now, however (thanks to the success of this experiment in acclimatisation), they offer abundance of grayling; and from their superabundance are being drawn the stocks which are enriching the other fishing waters of Scotland."

Mr. Piscator's account of the experiments was highly interesting. The first was made in December, 1855, when three dozen fish were brought by rail from Rowsley, Derbyshire, in the first Eyre's fish-carrier ever used. Mr. Piscator described with enthusiasm the exultation with which their almost unhoped-for safe arrival was greeted, and the delight which he experienced when, with his own

* See "The Field," Nov. 24, 1860.

hands, he committed his finny guests to the waters of the Clyde, the first graylings that had ever swam in Scottish waters. This experiment was afterwards supplemented by obtaining a quantity of ova, and hatching them in boxes set in a small stream conveniently connected with a breeding pond, and so into the Clyde. The arrangement of this pond and stream is so simple and convenient for the purpose of carrying out similar experiments, that we give a diagram of it.

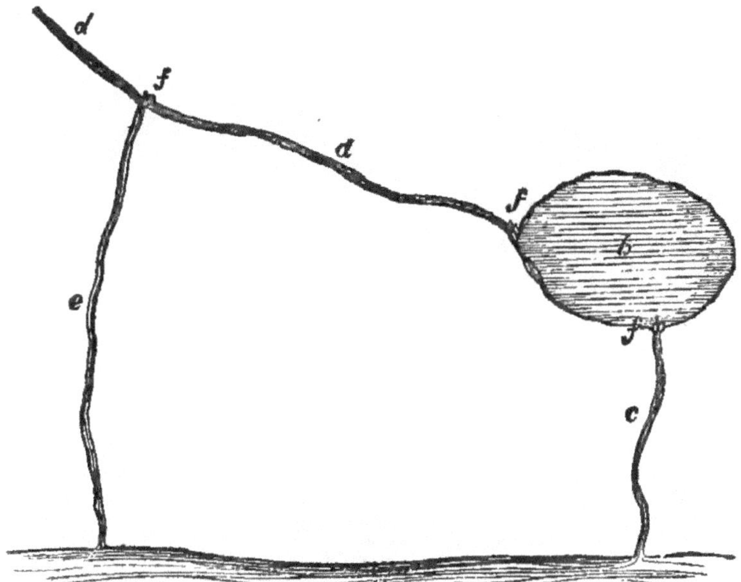

a The river Clyde.
b The pond.
c Outlet from pond into the Clyde.
d d Small stream down the side of the hill.
e Branch of same falling into the Clyde.
f f f Gates.

The ova were laid in a hatching-box in stream *d*, between the two gates; and by means of the channel *e*, and a proper use of the upper gate, the quantity of water could be so regulated as not to injure the ova. As the fish were hatched, they were let into the pond, and there kept and fed until of sufficient size to be entrusted to the perils of river life.

There can be no doubt at this moment, 1863, the grayling is firmly established in the Clyde, and that in a few years it will be found in most of the principal streams, thus materially adding to the angling resources of the country.

SALMON IN HANOVER SQUARE.

Page 217.

A ludicrous incident once took place with some of my young fish. On one occasion, when I had the honour of reading a paper on the subject before the Zoological Society, and after I and everybody had had our say—expressed our ideas, our fears, and our hopes on the subject—I proceeded to put a young trout under the microscope. When, however, I came to look at the fish, they were getting very faint, for the room was too hot for them. They were placed (some dozen of them) in a glass dish, in order that they might be easily seen by all. I therefore put away the microscope, not wishing to lose any of the fish, and gave the dish, with the fish in it, to my servant, telling him to go off immediately in a cab, and put them back in the cold fresh water of the hatching apparatus. Away he went directly; and a few minutes afterwards he returned into the room with a long face, holding in his hand the glass basin *empty*—water, fish, and all had suddenly gone. I was not obliged to wait long for an explanation. My servant told me that he had taken the fish down stairs when I gave them to him, and had placed them for a *moment* on the table in the hall while he went to fetch his hat from the hat room—he had not been gone one minute—when he came back and found the basin empty. He quickly found out the culprit; the civil (and in this case too attentive) hall porter, had seen the basin on his table, and thinking it did not look tidy, took it up then and there, deliberately walked to the street-door, and threw out bodily the contents—salmon, trout, charr, salmon-trout, eggs, young ones, and all—on to the pavement of the street.

He then went in again, and put the basin on his hall table. Immediately this was reported to me, I did not know whether to be angry or to laugh; however, "laughing had it." I turned out immediately with candles, camel-hair brushes, and spoons, and with the assistance of several gentlemen who happened to come out of the society rooms at the moment, set to work and picked up the gasping little wretches one by one. We were all groping about on our hands and knees in the semi-darkness, when a crowd (of course) collected. One of the spectators asked me what I was doing. "Catching salmon," said I. "Catching salmon in Hanover-square," said he, "good gracious; what next?" and away he went as fast as his legs would carry him, thinking doubtless he had come upon a party of midnight lunatics. If he sees this he may get the explanation he was then in too great a fright to wait for.

SALMON NETS.

Page 220.

The attention of Parliament has been chiefly directed to close seasons and nets. First and foremost, nets and paid engines (the angler's aversion)—nets in all forms, shapes, and sizes—nets half as long as Regent-street, and as deep as the first-floor windows are high—nets placed across the rivers like the hurdles across the much-worn paths in Hyde Park—day nets, night nets, and nets that fish by themselves day and night. Imagine Rotten Row a salmon stream, the good citizens salmon. Four P.M., the spate and the fish running up, a great net is spread at the three arches at Hyde Park-corner, another great net from the statue to the Duke's house, nets half way across the Row every fifty yards, and every now and then a wall with nets in the gaps; add to this, fierce and cunning ogres fishing for us from the walk with rods and hooks baited with devices the most tempting to our nature. How many of us would get up to Kensington Gardens, where, all collected there listening to the band, suddenly from the tree-tops is let down a large net, and the assembled crowd encircled with its lethal meshes, and taken out like a net of cabbages out of a kitchen boiler; even suppose a few did escape, and imagine the young fish coming down again from the Gardens to the sea (which we will call Piccadilly), the innocents would be stopped short by the nets, and caught by the rods; they would be knocked on the head by the wheels (mill-wheels); one out of a thousand would get away safely. Rotten Row would soon become depopulated, Kensington Gardens spawnless, and the race extinct; the ogres would give up preserving our race.*

PERCH AND GOLD FISH.

Both perch and gold fish can be hatched in boxes. Perch spawn may be found at the end of April or beginning of May hanging on to the bushes or weeds by the water side, or it may be obtained by the plan hit upon by my friend Captain Berkely, 2nd Life Guards, who writes me thus:—"I have found out a good plan of securing perch spawn, and a more natural one. Set a bow-net alongside weeds, with a red flower at the bottom of it; the perch will come in, and if left quietly in it, will hang their strings of ova to the cross-strings and all over the net. One morning I got a pint pot quite full from the perch which had gone in, picking it off the strings. The net had been left set in the lake for three days and three nights."

The spawn of gold fish may be collected from the weeds on which they deposit it, or it may be taken

* See article on salmon by myself, "Household Words," July 20, 1861. Excellent models of these nets have been deposited by the Fisheries Preservation Association in the South Kensington Museum.

from them by the same method as is applied to salmon and trout.*

I have hatched out from the egg many thousand young perch. The water should be *just* flowing,—a rapid stream is not required. I obtained my stock principally from the Thames, where the spawn (that is, what the swans had left of it) could, a week or ten days ago (May 9th), be seen hanging to the boughs and bushes like masses of jelly. I have, moreover, some spawn which I have taken from the fish, and treated after the usual manner, well known to pisciculturists. Now, this perch spawn is very peculiar; it is found in the form of long ribbons. This, the reader may possibly think, is no news. But let us examine it a little closer, and we shall find it is really a beautiful structure. In the first place we shall find, on close examination, that the ribbon is *hollow;* for if a couple of inches or so be cut off the length of the spawn and floated in water, it can be spread out in the form of a ring, about five or six inches in diameter. Again, if the observer be very neat-handed, a thin stick, or a whalebone rib of an old umbrella, can be passed down the whole length of the ribbon, which can thus be threaded on the stick like a footless stocking on to a mop-handle. This *hollow* ribbon is composed entirely of a mass of eggs, and these we find to be arranged in a most remarkable manner. There is now a portion of the spawn floating in pure water before me, and it resembles exactly the pattern of an old-fashioned long silk purse, or of a

* See Mr. A. Smee's admirable book on "Reason and Instinct." Bohn, Covent Garden.

lady's hair-net; that is to say, the eggs are arranged in rings. Each ring unites, without any interval, at the point of contact with its neighbouring ring, so as to form a really exceedingly pretty and highly ornamental pattern, well worthy of the art-designers—if those gentlemen will only leave off *imagining* patterns, and take a lesson or two from nature.

As we gently pull the perch spawn from off the bough on which it has been deposited by the parent fish, we shall find that it is highly elastic, and, if extended, will recoil upon itself like a bell-spring. Why is this? The ribbon, apparently continuous, like a strip of calico, is not really so. Not only is it double in structure, but it is arranged in folds upon itself. Reader, take a paper spill from the fireplace, fold it up closely from end to end upon itself, and then put it on the table. It will partially straighten itself, and you will have a rude model of the cause of the elasticity of perch spawn.

My friend, Mr. King, of Watford, brought me some perch spawn on the 20th of April, which had been deposited by the fish in his pond on the 19th. It was placed in my boxes, and the young fish could be seen moving in the egg on the 23rd, and they were all hatched out by the 26th. When the fish begin to move in the egg, the appearance is most curious—the whole mass of spawn seems alive and in quick and rapid motion, an appearance caused by each fish moving and kicking in its own private apartment. Why they move so continuously I know not; anyhow, they twist and wriggle about without a moment's intermission, and, what is very remarkable, their object seems to be to make a complete tour round their egg, for they most certainly manage to perform the circuit in about four or five quick and flea-like motions, and they continue at this work all day long. When hatched out, the little perch are so minute and so transparent that it is almost impossible to see them unless there are a number congregated together. Hundreds were washed away with the water through the perforated zinc; but hundreds were hatched every day to supply their place. Not liking to lose all these fish, I turned them into the salmon and trout boxes, and was pleased to find that these fish would feed famously on the young perch; and many a fine course has taken place in the tanks, the trout pursuing the young perch like a greyhound a hare. These voracious young creatures will also hunt and catch any young grayling that comes down into their tank, but they like the young perch the best. I have no idea how these young perch manage to exist when born in their native ponds or rivers: they are so exceedingly minute and delicate, that I should think *everything* would eat them. Not only this; but, even if not eaten, I find that they will die at the slightest provocation, and it is on this account difficult to rear them, or even to keep them alive very long.

PURIFYING PONDS.

The great difficulty in the management of ponds seems to be the fact that they so soon become filled with mud, &c. A correspondent of "the Field,"

Mr. John Grant, bas suggested the following remedy, which I trust may be found to work well. He has kindly allowed me to introduce it into my little book :—

" Sir,—Public attention has for a long time been directed to purifying the water in large ponds and reservoirs ; and, as I have lately succeeded in effecting this desirable object in a fishpond about 10 feet deep, the following sketch will enable the public to profit by it.

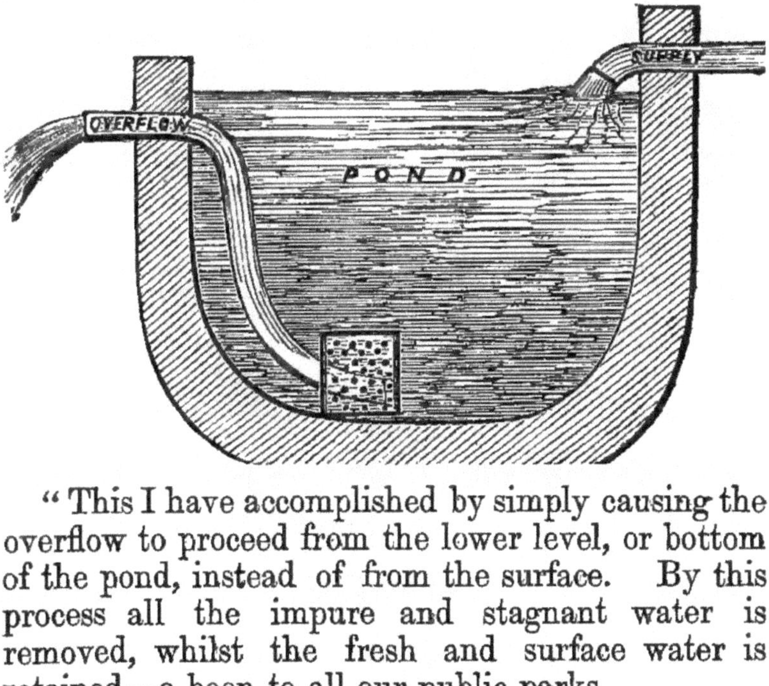

" This I have accomplished by simply causing the overflow to proceed from the lower level, or bottom of the pond, instead of from the surface. By this process all the impure and stagnant water is removed, whilst the fresh and surface water is retained—a boon to all our public parks.

" JOHN GRANT."

" Hyde Park Street, March 30."

As I have been often asked what books on the science of Pisciculture have been published, I have given for the benefit of my readers as complete a list as I can.

1. Voyage D'Exploration sur le Littoral de la France et de L'Italie. Par M. Coste. Paris, Imprimerie Imperiale.

This treats on the cultivation of oysters and the breeding of eels. It is a magnificent but expensive book.

2. Instructions Pratiques sur la Pisciculture suivies de memoires et de Rapports, sur la meme sujet. Par M. Coste. Paris, Librairie de Victor Masson, 17, Place de L'Ecole-de-Medecine.

3. Pisciculture Pratique, Considerations Generales et Pratiques sur le Repeuplement des eaux de la France. Par M. G. Millet. Bordeaux, G. Gounouilhou, Imprimeur de l'Academie Imperiale, Place Puy-Paulin.

4. Pisciculture Pratique, Rapport sur les mesures a prendre pour Assurer le Repeuplement des Cours d'eau de la France. Par M. G. Millet. Paris, au Siege de la Société, Rue de Lille, 19, Hôtel Lauraquais.

5. Pisciculture, Rapport sur le Repeuplement des Cours d'eau et sur les travaux de pisciculture de M. Millet. Paris, Librairie Centrale D'Agriculture et de Jardinage, Quai des Grands Augustins 41. Auguste Goin, Editeur.

6. Pisciculture: Considerations Generales et Pratiques sur la Pisciculture Marine. Par M. G. Millet. Paris, Imprimerie de G.-B. Gros et Donnaud, Son Gendre, Rue des Noyers 74.

7. Pisciculture: Observations sur la communication verbale de M. Coste. Par M. Millet. Paris, Simon Raçon et Comp., Rue d'Erfurth 1.

8. Notice Historique sur l'Etablissement de Pisciculture de Huningue. Strasbourg, Imprimerie de Veuve Levrault, 1862.

9. Rapport sur la Pisciculture et les Pêches Fluviales en Angleterre, en Ecosse et en Irlande, au double point de vue des Procedes de Production tant Naturel, Qu' artificiel, &c. Strasbourg, Imprimerie de Veuve Berger Levrault, 1863. The result of M. Coume's official visit to this country.

10. Treatise on the Propagation of Salmon and other Fish. By Edmund and Thomas Ashworth. Stockport: printed by E. H. King, Bridge-street. Simpkin and Marshall, London. 1*s.*

11. The Natural History of the Salmon as ascertained by the recent experiments in the Artificial Spawning and Hatching of the Ova, and rearing of the Fry, at Stormontfield, on the Tay. By W. Brown. Glasgow, Thomas Murray and Son; Edinburgh, Paton and Ritchie; London, Arthur Hall, Virtue and Co. 2*s.* 6*d.*

12. Fish Culture. By Francis Francis. London: Routledge, Warne, and Routledge, 2, Farringdon-street; New York, 56, Walker-street. 5*s.*

13. Supplementary Report on the Rivers of Spain and Portugal. Manchester: Love and Barton, Printers, Market-street.

14. The Salmon and its Artificial Propagation. By Robert Ramsbottom, Clitheroe. London; Simpkin, Marshall and Co. Stationers' Hall-court; Manchester, Johnson and Rawson, 89, Market-street; and all booksellers.

15. Translation of the Proceedings of the French Pisciculturists. By W. H. Fry. Published by Appleton, of New York.

16. Artificial Spawning, Breeding, and Rearing of Fish. By Gottlieb Boecius. Van Voorst, Paternoster-row. 7*s.* 6*d.*

THE END.

CPSIA information can be obtained
at www.ICGtesting.com
Printed in the USA
LVHW101650140522
718424LV00010B/225

9 783375 006839